THE NEW GIRL
NEXT DOOR

LAURA BURTON

COPYRIGHT

Written in U.S. English

First Edition

Edited by Tochi Biko

Proofed by Vanda O'Neill

1

CHESSY

"Happy birthday, Chessy! I can't believe our baby sister is thirty now."

"Don't, you're making me feel old."

I'm on a three-way call with my older sisters, Leila and Lucy. As usual, they're fussing. I smile to myself.

"Have you got a bucket list?" Leila asks. Before I can reply, Lucy butts in.

"You should add a trip to New Zealand. I can't even begin to tell you how beautiful it is here."

I sigh, picturing Lucy and Wyatt—Lucy's fiancé—hiking in lush green mountains, probably dressed up in Lord of the Rings cosplay. I almost chuckle out loud at the thought of several Arwen and Aragorn couples wandering around Hobbiton right now.

Lucy is so lucky to have found a man willing to do fun things like that with her.

"How is Wyatt treating you?" I ask, swooning at the thought of a man sweeping me off my feet and taking me somewhere fancy.

Lucy doesn't reply right away, giving Leila the perfect opportunity to insert her thoughts. "How do you think he's treating her? The girl found herself a billionaire who is just as crazy about geeky stuff as she is. And soon, they're going to get married! At the Plaza hotel, no less."

"You make it sound like I won the lottery. Like it was easy. It wasn't. And planning a wedding is stressful."

My smile grows at the sound of irritation in Lucy's voice, and my attention wanders to my empty apartment as my sisters start to bicker.

"...and anyway, you can talk. Blaze isn't exactly poor, is he? Didn't he just order himself a new Bugatti?"

There's a pause, and I can just picture Leila's face growing red while she does a lot of rapid blinking. Things will escalate if I don't chime in, and the last thing I want right now is to listen to my sisters argue.

"Cut it out, you two. It's my birthday. Leila, you're still in the country. Fancy going out?"

There's a big, breathy sigh as Leila inhales another sharp breath. Her puffy red cheeks flash through my mind's eye.

"Sorry, Chessy, the doctor put me on bed rest until I have the twins," she confesses, sounding pained.

I'm not super surprised. The last time I saw her, she was in full waddle mode. A few steps made her break into a sweat.

I can't deny I'm disappointed, though. Before my sisters settled down, we always went out on my birthday. And this one is a big one.

"Shoot. Well, I can come and take care of you!" I offer, thinking that at least we can eat junk food and watch our favorite *Friends* episodes in bed.

"Actually, Blaze is home and he's—"

I fail to stop a groan from escaping me. The last thing I want to be on my thirtieth birthday is the third wheel.

Being in the same room as Blaze and Leila has become even more nauseating lately. You'd think a high-risk pregnancy would calm him down, but surprisingly, the man can't keep his hands off Leila's pregnant curves and takes every opportunity to grope her.

I'm all about romance and that, but as a bystander, it's gross.

"Sorry, Chessy." Lucy's voice makes me jump. I forgot she was even on the call. She'd been so quiet for the last few minutes. "We'll celebrate when I get back, I promise."

"No worries. I'll speak to you guys later."

I pretend to be cheerful as I end the call, not wanting my sisters to know how let down I feel.

As the baby sister of three girls, I can't help the need I feel to please people. And I spend a lot of my energy manifesting my dreams.

Well, I used to spend time manifesting.

Now… Not so much.

Until recently, I haven't had a reason to think I won't get everything I want out of life.

Then my last boyfriend stole from me—a new low.

And I'm not talking metaphorically here. He didn't steal my heart or anything. No. He took my wallet instead.

The worst part? He did it at a family BBQ,

giving everyone a good show of what a low life he is. My brother-in-law kicked his butt right in front of everyone. I looked like a joke.

My older sisters have always disapproved of how fast I jump into relationships. After that episode, they think I suck at character judgment too.

But I refuse to stay down about it for too long —Leila and Lucy have made monumental changes in their lives and their dreams are coming true.

If they can find their happy endings, so can I. I know it, deep down.

Tonight, though, I can't help but let in a little anxiety about "what if?"

Leila is about to have two adorable babies, and Lucy is off with her fiancé on a month-long Lord of the Rings-themed vacation.

Then there's me.

I never thought I'd make it to thirty without a few kids running around my feet and a sexy husband by my side. But here I am, leaning over my breakfast bar and staring at a lowly cupcake with a single candle and too much frosting. I light a match and watch the flame for several long seconds. The wax drips slowly toward the frosting.

In so many ways, I feel like that candle. My heart sinks even lower. I'm not getting any younger, and all I've ever wanted in life is to meet the man of my dreams and fill our huge house with adorable kids.

"Happy birthday, Chessy," I say, blowing out the candle.

I don't bother to make a wish.

It's not all bad, I try to tell myself. I have my dream job, working as a kindergarten teacher in a good school. I mean, sure, the staffroom smells like coffee and BO, the bathroom floor is always suspiciously wet, and someone keeps parking in my space, so I have to snake around the busy parking lot to find another one. The principal kind of scares me, too. Plus, her son is in my class, which adds to the pressure. Luckily though, he's sweet. And that's a silver lining, isn't it?

In fact, the kids in my class are amazing.

Another pro to my job is that I have my very own classroom with the freedom to decorate it with all the fingerprint artwork I like, to make my heart happy.

There are also all those bright, beaming smiles I get to see on those kids' faces every day. They flood my heart with so much joy.

But right now, I'm alone in my cold apartment on my thirtieth birthday. Reality brings a sigh to my lips.

It's Friday night.

I should put on my red dress, slap on a bold lipstick, and go out.

Enthusiasm bubbles briefly, then fizzles.

I look down at my bunny slippers, stretchy leggings, and oversized T-shirt. My dirty blonde hair in a messy bun at the top of my head.

What has become of me?

I've turned into Lucy. She's the comfort-over-fashion kind of person.

I'm usually the type to devour fashion magazines and, on the weekend, spend a happy eight hours going from store to store, trying everything on.

But ever since I moved to the city, my bank has maintained a resounding no to everything fun.

I pick up my phone and check my balance again. Another huff escapes me. "I can't even afford a freaking birthday cake," I mutter aloud.

Sure, I have my dream job and I live in my favorite city in the world. But New York prices are sky high compared to New Jersey, and kindergarten teachers don't get paid enough to eat, let alone do anything with their lives.

In fact, I took the stipend for medical and put it toward my rent instead. Now I'm nervous when I get so much as a paper cut, because I won't be able to afford the doctor's appointment, let alone antibiotics for an infection.

I glance at the bulging sack spilling over the top of the trash can and shake my head, snapping myself out of a downward spiral.

It's my birthday. I'm not going to have a pity party in my dark, empty apartment.

My party-girl, free-spirited days are over. I'm in my thirties now, and I need to start being responsible. Starting with taking out the trash.

I tie the sack and carry it out into the hall, while I try to think up a plan to celebrate. A cheap one—so my bank balance doesn't dip any further into the red.

It'll most likely be one that involves consuming the last of the vanilla ice-cream in my freezer and a Netflix binge-athon.

I stuff the trash into the shoot and turn back to my apartment, my mind a million miles away, and my forehead collides with something hard.

Or someone.

"Will you look where you're going?" the someone growls.

I stop rubbing my head and quickly open my eyes.

I recognize that deep, rumbly voice.

A pair of blue eyes bore into mine. I take in a square jaw, a bulging bottom lip, and a mouth positioned in a straight line.

Goosebumps break out on my neck, and I resist the urge to swoon.

His dark brows knit together, and he looks me over with the most unimpressed stare.

I flash him a nervous smile. "Sorry," I blurt before my brain can remind me I'm not supposed to like this guy. "Didn't see you there."

My heart is hammering in my chest and my palms are sweaty. It's just like every other time I've set eyes on him.

This is the one person in the world who hates me, and I have no idea what I've done to deserve it.

He also happens to be the one guy in the world who can still make me weak at the knees, despite my plan to swear off men for the foreseeable future.

He blinks. My gaze flickers to the two trash

bags in his hands. I jump out of the way and fold my arms while he proceeds to dispose of them. Then he turns back, and I watch him take in my appearance. *Ugh.*

Suddenly, I can no longer hear my hammering heart. It's like I'm having an out of body experience.

This is the last person I would want to bump into in my bunny slippers. I should be in my best dress and heels, with my hair curled so it's hanging in mermaid waves over my body.

Maybe then he wouldn't be looking at me like I'm something sticky under his shoe.

Is he really still mad about the last time we met? Annoyance builds up inside of me and I let a frown take over my polite smile.

"Why do you have to be like that?" I mumble, frowning a little. "I apologized. I don't know where you're from, but here it's customary to forgive someone when they say they're sorry."

He snorts and rakes a hand through his dark hair. My brain races to find a list of reasons why I shouldn't have a crush on this guy.

His white shirt lifts just enough for me to get a sneak peek at his tanned, muscled torso. I meet his eyes again, feeling a flush of heat to my cheeks. I hope he didn't notice me checking him out.

I mean, the man is intolerable, but I'm a red-blooded woman who can notice a hot guy when she sees one. Even if he is an alpha hole.

"You're right," he says, folding his arms. His shoulder muscles bulge like mountains. My brows lift in surprise.

"I am?" I ask, popping a hip and twirling my hair now. I sense his apology for being rude to me is just on the tip of his tongue. Maybe I had him all wrong. Maybe this guy is actually—

"You *don't* know where I'm from. And where I'm from, we don't automatically forgive people when they've been obnoxious. Especially after they've been violent."

I drop my arms along with my jaw. "Excuse me?"

The cheek of this guy! I can't even.

He points to a pink mark on his forehead and my stomach tightens. Did I make that mark?

Then the guy drops his hands with a deflated puff.

"Listen, it's been a murder of a week for me, and I already had a headache," he explains.

I resist the urge to apologize again. I don't

want to be that woman. But my wounded puppy radar starts screaming at me and I'm flooded with an empathy that has me working on autopilot. I cock my head to the side. "Aww," I coo. "That's too bad."

The guy's jaw bulges and his eyes flash. I watch him in confused silence as he strides back to his door, which is across from mine. But then he stops, and his shoulders drop a notch. He lets out an audible breath. "I don't mean to snap at you," he says, keeping his back to me.

My heart flutters, sensing the agony in his voice. It's as though every word is cutting him on the way out of his mouth.

He turns to face me and holds out a hand. I eye it, frozen on the spot for a moment. When I don't take it, he adds, "I'm Jack."

I study him carefully for a moment, then I take his hand and we shake. His grip is firm and his fingers are calloused, grazing my palm as we break away.

"Chessy," I say, my mouth already dry.

Oh no.

My hopeless romantic body is lighting up with all sorts of forbidden signals again. Sweaty palms. Fluttery heart. Short breaths.

I hear Lucy's firm voice in my head. *Get a grip, Chessy*.

Jack's mouth lifts into a lopsided smile. "I know."

"Know what?" I ask like a fool. Why do I always turn into a pile of goo around guys? Honestly, the second a man shows me any attention, I'm putty in their hands.

A shrink would probably blame it on daddy issues. Or in my case, absent-daddy issues.

Jack laughs and it jerks me out of my daze. "You've told me before," he says.

He's talking about the last time we spoke. It was months ago. When Wyatt proposed to Lucy —down on one knee right here in the hall like his soul couldn't bear to wait a single moment longer before he popped the question. It was so romantic!

Jack came out demanding that we keep the noise down.

"You remember," I say, unable to hide the admiration in my voice.

My reaction doesn't go unnoticed. Jack's smile drops and he clears his throat, turning serious again.

"Well, have a good night," he says. His gaze

flickers to my shirt at the last minute, and I suck in a breath, realizing I'm not wearing a bra. Is he checking me out?

"And happy birthday," he adds, meeting my eyes again.

I look down at my shirt and spot the pin. One of the kids from my class gave it to me in the morning. It's shaped like a pink balloon with the words "it's my birthday" written across it.

I flush and smile back. "Thanks."

I make a beeline for my door before I can do anything else to embarrass myself, but instead of storming into my apartment, I headbutt the jammed door instead.

"Ouch!"

I hold my head, my ears ringing. A pair of warm hands is suddenly on my arms. I'm swiveled around and two concerned eyes study my face. Seafoam blue eyes. "That was quite a bump, are you alright?" Jack asks. His face is so close to mine, I can taste the mint on his breath. My stomach flips again.

"I'm fine. Just clumsy," I say with a giggle. I fumble with the door handle until I hear a click, then ram my butt against the door to force it open.

This time, the door obeys and swings open with a jarring squeal. My head is thumping as I offer Jack a grin, then I take two steps back into my apartment and let the door slam shut.

"You should probably put some ice on that," Jack shouts through the door, his voice muffled.

"Thanks for the tip," I yell, wanting to die from the embarrassment. I turn the lock and listen for the sound of Jack's door closing. When I hear it shut, I let out a breath.

Then I spin around and survey my quiet apartment. It's meticulously clean, with pretty pink and white cushions propped up on the couch. My phone and the remote sit in a neat line on the glass coffee table, and the only source of light is the soft, yellow glow coming from my bedroom down the hall.

Forget watching *Friends*, it's like I just stumbled right into an episode. I'm no longer in the mood for junk food and TV. I pick up a bottle of red and head for my room.

2

JACK

There are several reasons why I shouldn't drink tonight. None of those seem to matter as I pour myself another glass of malt whiskey.

I down the drink in one and my insides relax. The smoky taste reminds me of sitting by the campfire with my dad in years gone by.

My chest heaves a breath of its own accord at the thought of my dad. This is how I know the drink is working—my inner filter is lax.

Usually, I keep memories and thoughts of my dad in a box with big straps to bind it shut. That box should be in one of the deeper crevices of my mind.

The reason? Thinking about him brings me

too much pain. It's like ripping open a scar, then pouring salt into the wound.

But the whiskey is making my head spin. The contents of my mind are one jumbled mess. The box is open and a few of those forbidden thoughts are spilling out.

I glance at the grandfather clock standing by the door. It's almost one in the morning. I know I should head to bed, but my feet are glued to the floor.

If my mom was here, she'd give me one of her disapproving looks with her thin arms folded. She wouldn't say it, but I know she'd be thinking that I'm being irresponsible.

My mood sinks even lower as I think about my parents. After all these years, I can still remember the dark hairs on my dad's fingers and the way they curved like half-moons. I can picture the scar he had near his left ear too, from the time he fell off his bike and caught a tree branch on the way down.

He used to keep his hair long and shaggy to cover it up. But I knew it was there.

He always smelled like a campfire, and he would keep his sunglasses on as long as he could before Mom nagged him to take them off. I always wondered why. His eyes were so beautiful —green with flecks of brown.

And my mom. I remember her eyes would grow misty every time she looked at him.

I pour another glass, and my hand begins to tremble. I started drinking to drown out the pain. But the alcohol is sharpening the sting tonight.

I try one more time with another swig. The liquid burns an oaky trail down my throat.

My heart continues to throb.

Desperate to feel numb, I pour another drink. The glass is at my lips when I hear a thump. I pause.

My ears prick up. Did I imagine the noise? After a few moments, there's another thump.

I set down my glass, push my chair back, and wince at the jarring noise. When I open my door, the last person I expect to see is standing in front of me.

"You know it's my birthday," Chessy says, lifting a half empty bottle of wine. Her pink cheeks tell me that the bottle was probably full an hour ago. Her hair is tied up in a loose bun that is wobbling at the very top of her head as she leans against my doorframe.

She looks cuter than usual. Her baggy shirt is

half tucked into a pair of tight leggings and she's not got a lick of make up on. The red in her cheeks is the only color on her face.

She gives me a heady look, then her eyes move to my left and I glance back at the open bottle of whiskey and glass on the countertop, in plain sight.

When I return my gaze to Chessy, she's looking at me almost triumphantly.

"There's an old saying that goes, 'Nobody should drink alone.'" She winks. "So, what do you say?"

I chew my tongue as I think on it.

Chessy is a pretty woman, sure. It's not that I haven't noticed her narrow waist and the shapely swell of her hips. Not to mention, her current attire is leaving little to the imagination, making my brain concoct all kinds of inappropriate thoughts.

But her happy-go-lucky attitude is the biggest turn off. No one can be that happy all the time.

There's something about her mood tonight, though… She's got a smile planted on her face, but it doesn't quite reach her eyes.

Maybe it's the alcohol making me look at things in a weird way. But I swear I sense a note of sadness. I step aside to let her in. "They also say, 'Misery loves company,'" I add as she walks inside my apartment.

She chuckles. "What gave me away?"

I bite my lip to stop myself from making a sarcastic remark. It's her birthday. But instead of going out with friends or her crazy loud sisters, she's intoxicated, alone, and coming onto me. I decide to pivot to the minor bump she had earlier.

"How's the head?"

She waves a hand as though to bat the question away, and I watch her strut to the drink on the counter. Her body is so squishy in all the right places, it makes me break into a sweat.

I force my expression to stay neutral when she looks at me, hoping she isn't a mind reader.

I'm not sure what Chessy would do if she could read my thoughts. She'd either slap me and leave or come on heavy and hard. I'm not sure I like either of those options, although one of them sounds considerably more appealing than the other.

She looks at me with her brows raised as she picks up the whiskey bottle. "You can tell a lot about a man by his drink."

I join her at the breakfast bar and incline my

head, intrigued. "Is that so?" I grab a spare glass and hand it to Chessy, who pours herself a small drink. She picks it up and swirls the liquid as she appears to think on it.

"A man whose signature drink is whiskey is mature." Her eyes dart in my direction and I can tell that her inhibitions are gone. Her gaze dips to my mouth for a flicker of a moment. "A deep thinker."

I raise my brows. "You're not wrong there," I say, picking up my glass.

Chessy's cheeks dimple and her eyes sparkle with delight at my affirmation. She reaches for my arm and her nails graze my bicep. "He's strong, but not in a big-muscle kind of way. He's stubborn…"

"I prefer determined."

Chessy flashes me her teeth, then gulps down her drink. I nod to her.

"What does red wine say about a person?" I ask, suddenly aware of how close her knee is to mine. A flood of heat rushes through me.

Chessy arches her back, rolls her shoulders back, and sighs. "People who drink red are more adventurous, promiscuous…"

I cock a brow at her. Even in my intoxicated

state, I can tell she's tipsier than I am. "Promiscuous?"

Chessy pulls out her bun, letting her hair fall around her shoulders. Then she wraps a strand around her finger and her eyes dip to my lips a second time.

All of the heat in my body travels south.

There's a tiny voice in my head telling me we're in dangerous territory right now.

She might consider herself promiscuous, but I am not.

I don't just jump into bed with someone I hardly know. Especially these days. The ink is barely dry on my divorce papers, for one thing. Now every time I see the opposite sex, I'm tormented by a barrage of thoughts. She might be the next woman to grip my heart in a vice and squeeze until nothing comes out. Or she might be better for me.

What if I can never get past the trauma of this divorce? What if I end up dying alone?

She's right, I *am* a deep thinker.

I must write extensive pro/con lists before making any big decisions. Yet, now, my hand is reaching for her hair all on its own. Against my better judgment, I take a fistful, and discover that her locks are velvet soft. A waft of her scent hits me and all my senses come alive.

She smells like strawberries and cream—sweet and milky.

It's both illustrious and alarming.

She's like a honey trap. I lean in, and Chessy's pretty eyes grow big.

Our noses hover an inch apart from each other

"Yes," she whispers. "And we believe in true love."

"True love is just a fairy tale," I murmur against her mouth. Buttery lips touch mine for a second and a rush of tingles scatter through my body. My hands flex at my sides. I want to grip those delicious curves.

Suddenly, this woman is climbing onto my lap, and her weight on my hips is the most delightful kind of agony. There's a fire ablaze in me now, and I forget this is highly inappropriate behavior.

Chessy is the new girl next door. The annoyingly chirpy, 'life is great' woman who probably has a bed full of Disney plushies in her apartment.

The way she sees the world is so far removed from how I see it, there's no way we could be compatible. And even if we are somehow made for each other, I'm not the type of man who gets drunk and sleeps with his new neighbor to celebrate his divorce.

Oddly, all of that seems to just float through my mind as my hands find a grip on her waist. Her warmth is like a healing balm. I realize I haven't felt the ache of my heart since she walked in. With a few touches, she has me more intoxicated than a whole bottle of whiskey.

I lift her onto the counter and nestle myself between her thighs.

The next thing I know, Chessy's hands are roaming through my hair and she's whispering in my ear. "Maybe you're right. Maybe true love isn't real. But this is…"

My eyes close of their own accord when she kisses me, and for the first time in months, my thoughts fade away.

Her mouth tastes dark and bitter. I lose myself in her, and all sense of time as we wrap ourselves around each other. Hands exploring, lips devouring. Face, neck, earlobe. Fingertips.

Her body fits snug against mine. I press her even closer. It may be the drink skewing my judgment, but I swear this is the most sensual kiss I've ever experienced.

When we finally break apart, Chessy starts to undo the buttons of my shirt. I almost moan.

Then her nails graze my bare chest and I'm suddenly smacked with a sense of reason.

I grip her arms, holding her still.

"I'm sorry," I say, lifting her off the counter and back onto the chair. "I can't do this."

Chessy's smile fades. "Do what?"

I gesture between us. "Whatever this is… It doesn't feel right."

I dig my nails into my palms as I head for my door. I yank it open when I reach it. "I think you need to go to bed."

Chessy's pretty lips pout at me. For a second, I think she's going to argue, but she tucks a strand of hair behind her ear, hops off the chair, and makes her way to the door instead. A part of me is disappointed. I was holding on to my self-control by a thread, and in the absence of her body I can already feel the sadness beginning to seep back in.

She turns around in the doorway, and a shiny tear rolls down her cheek. "Being alone on my birthday feels wrong too," she says, hugging herself.

My resolve wobbles. But I inwardly shake myself. This woman deserves more than a sloppy one-night stand with her newly divorced neighbor. She doesn't want to remember her thirtieth birthday as the one night she made a massive mistake and slept with the grumpy guy next door.

"Happy birthday, Chessy," I say, forcing a smile. She flushes as I give her a kiss on the cheek. "Now, go to bed. And I'll see you around."

I don't have it in me to say I'll see her in the morning, or any time soon. Because once the sun rises and we've sobered up, I'm pretty sure horror and humiliation will kick in. Then we'll be avoiding each other for a few weeks.

Chessy nods, but the look of devastation on her face is unmistakable. I curl my hand into a tight fist and grit my teeth, wrestling with the primal desire to do something highly inappropriate. It doesn't matter how much we both want it.

After a lingering look, Chessy sighs and walks across the hall to her apartment.

I'm just silently congratulating my restraint when Chessy gives her door a kick and slumps to the floor with a tiny wail.

I shut my eyes tight and try to contain my frustration. Then I look at her again.

"What's wrong?"

Chessy's face is buried in her hands, and I can barely make out her muffled reply. "I've locked myself out."

I pinch the bridge of my nose and take a sharp breath as the room begins to spin. My resolve is crumbling, but I use the last of my strength to scoop up Chessy and carry her back to my apartment. "What are you doing?" she asks, as I kick the door shut behind me. I stagger toward my room, hoping that my arms don't fail me and drop the beautiful woman. She gasps as I enter my room. Stepping over the threshold makes me feel absurdly like a husband carrying his new wife. Then I meet her wide eyes and growl four words, "Putting you to bed."

3

———

CHESSY

The obnoxious sound of my ringtone startles me awake with the most throbbing headache I've ever had. Groaning, I beat my phone into silence with a fist, then roll over and huff into my pillow.

An unfamiliar scent floods my nostrils and I cough at the musty smell. That's not my pillow.

My eyes are slits as I pull away to breathe fresh air.

It takes me a hot minute to register the fact that I'm not in my room.

I roll onto my back and clutch my temples, willing the ceiling to stop moving. My ears are ringing like an old kettle on the stove. "I'm never drinking again," I moan.

"Me neither," a deep voice replies. I jump so violently, I almost fall off the bed.

"Jack?" I ask, recognizing the voice trailing in through the open door.

My grumpy neighbor appears in the doorway and leans against the frame. He's wearing nothing but a pair of thin shorts that hang just above his knee. His tanned muscles are on full display and his dark hair is damp and dewy. It could be my imagination, but I swear the man is so hot he's steaming. He looks like he just stepped out of the shower.

"What are you doing in my room?" I blurt, unable to hide the horror in my voice. Jack's thick brows lift at my question, but he doesn't reply. I glance around me and remember I'm not in my apartment. I'm in his.

"Do you have any recollection of last night's events?" he asks, sounding mildly amused. I can't figure out what's so funny.

His gaze drops to my chest. I follow his gaze and discover I'm wearing a man's shirt.

It seems to match the color and style of his shorts.

"Is this yours?" I ask, yanking on the only piece of clothing that is keeping me modest.

For the first time ever, Jack's eyes seem to twinkle at me. I clutch the sheets and pull them up to my chin. "Oh my gosh. No. Please tell me we didn't…"

"We didn't," Jack cuts in, dropping his arms and standing straight. He clears his throat. "You were drunk."

"So were you," I reply, defensive. As though that makes it any better. My brain hurts as I try to remember. I catch a glimpse of my clothes, carefully folded and left in a neat pile on a chair in the corner of the room. There's a small ray of morning light falling on it through the open blinds.

A vague memory pops into my head—Jack folding the clothes and putting them there, while I giggled and made bed angels in my underwear. He turned and yanked off his shirt and tossed it to me, telling me to put it on.

Then he walked out of the room without a single glance back.

I clamp a hand over my open mouth at the memory. "I'm so sorry," I say into my palm.

Jack's brows are knitted together as he waves a hand aside. "Forget it. What are neighbors for?

I've already called a locksmith; he'll be here in an hour."

"Oh," is all I can say. There's an awkward silence as we avoid eye contact and stay frozen in our places. I'm still trying to figure out if I'm truly awake or if this is a crazy dream. I've been crushing on Jack ever since I moved into my apartment.

But if this was a dream, he'd be in bed with me. not standing in the doorway looking at me like I'm an intruder.

"I'll get dressed..." I say, motioning to my clothes. Jack needs to leave and let me shrink under the covers to die of embarrassment.

On cue, Jack mutters something inaudible and shuts the door. Now alone, I stuff a pillow over my face and scream.

How could I let myself be such a fool?

Why couldn't I be normal and watch TV until I passed out on my birthday? How will I ever face my neighbor again?

Maybe I should just move back to New Jersey and forget making a new life in the city.

After all, once I pay the locksmith, I'm officially out of money.

I scream into the pillow again as the realization hits me—I don't get paid until next week.

I'm in the middle of berating myself when a door squeals open again.

"Are you okay?"

Sheepish, I pull the pillow away and plaster a fake smile on my face. "Sure. This is just a morning ritual I do to psyche myself up for the day."

I meet Jack's skeptical gaze for a flicker of a moment, then let out a nervous laugh. I wonder what he sees when he looks at me.

Can he see through my breezy act to the insecure woman hiding in plain sight?

The corners of his mouth lift and I take a breath. My acting skills must be on point right now because I don't think he suspects a thing.

After getting dressed, I join Jack in his kitchen for a strong cup of coffee. We avert our gaze and keep the conversation light. I've never been very good at small talk, but today, I'm a pro.

I try not to stare as he leans over the breakfast bar with his elbows on the granite. He's thumbing through his phone, and he must be reading the news, because every now and then he comments on the headlines. But I find the news as interesting as watching paint dry. I just hum along and try to ignore the flashes of embarrassing memories from last night that keep coming at me.

We both jump at the sound of a knock on the door.

When the locksmith is gone, Jack smacks his lips together and ruffles a hand through his hair. "Well," he says, puffing out his cheeks. I tuck a strand of hair behind my ear and offer him a shy smile. "Thanks for putting me up," I say, hovering near my door. "I'm sorry for the way I behaved. I promise I'm not usually like that. I don't know what came over me." I heave an exaggerated sigh and run my fingers through my hair.

Jack's smile falters. "That's too bad," he says. He offers me a lopsided grin with a wink and my stomach does a standing backflip.

He folds his arms and leans on his doorframe.

I bite my lip.

I want to ask him what he meant by that, but the words fail to leave my mouth. I laugh instead, looking anywhere but at him. An awkward silence lingers.

Alright, then. I push my door shut. Just before the lock clicks, I hear him speak.

"Can I make a suggestion?"

I wrench open the door again to see his face, and my heart is fluttering like a butterfly. Jack steps forward, his shoulders rounded and expression intense. The air around me is suddenly warm. I swallow. "Sure?"

He searches my eyes, and I feel like I'm melting under his gaze. The man makes me feel naked. Vulnerable. Transparent. Like my soul is laid out bare for him to gaze upon.

All the romantic movies I've seen play out in my mind as I bask in the heat of his gaze, but then he opens his mouth and his words are like a flood of ice-cold water on my head.

"I think it's best we pretend last night never happened."

4

JACK

Monday rolls along too soon for comfort.

I feel empty inside, but the dull, throbbing ache in my temples persists.

I'm in a conference room, surrounded by the board of directors of Great Hospital in downtown New York. Charles, the Chief of Surgery, is seated next to me—his shiny black shoe tapping the table leg. I guess he's nervous for the both of us.

All eyes are on me. The air is heavy, but outside the long windows, I see birds swooping in the blue sky. My chest tightens as I watch them, trying to ignore what's happening inside the conference room. I've never envied a bird before now. I'd give all of my money to get away.

"It's been eight weeks, Jack."

My eyes return to Walter, the Great Hospital director. There are dark circles under his eyes and his waxy skin is taut over his cheekbones. He's giving me a stern look, and his fingers are laced together.

I know he's trying to intimidate me, but part of me wants to laugh. The man reminds me of Voldemort, and I've never been able to take him seriously at the best of times. Today is no different.

My mouth twitches, giving away my amusement. Walter starts berating me.

"Is this funny to you? The jury found you guilty of medical negligence. Now this hospital is under fire from the press. People want heads to roll."

I fold my hands and rest them on the glossy table as I clench my jaw. "Of course, I don't find this funny," I say, curt. I haven't found anything truly funny since the event.

I look to Charles and find his wrinkled eyes boring into me like hot lasers. I don't sense fury. Or even irritation. His foot has stopped tapping and his shoulders are slumped. There's disappointment written all over his tanned face. Somehow, that makes things worse.

I swallow a bubble of emotion and look away, my eyes prickling. "As I've said before. I apologize for putting everyone in this position. And I will resign immediately—"

I stop when Walter slams a palm on the table with a bang.

"For goodness' sake, Jack. We can't afford to lose another heart surgeon. You're the best in the state, and with you gone, we'll—"

"A patient died at my hand, Walter, I've been found guilty…" The words rip the back of my throat as I say them.

The sea of eyes directed at me suddenly fly in different directions as the room of men exchange looks.

Charles coughs and leans forward, presumably to try to reason with me. I know his job is to persuade me to return to work, but I can't think of anything more inappropriate. I should be locked away for what I did.

"The hospital has insurance for these cases. How long did you expect your winning streak to last, eh? It's the law of averages. You need to stop beating yourself up."

There's softness in his voice now, but it does not cover up the sound of desperation. I rise to my feet, grinding my teeth. "Hell will freeze over before I stop holding myself responsible for destroying that young family's happiness. And it was never about winning. Or awards. Or whatever else you want to call it. It's about knowing when to stop. I am a danger in that operating room. I'm not going back."

The men become restless in their chairs. A few people mutter to one another, and I get a strong sense I'm not the only person in the room who thinks I shouldn't see the light of day again.

"All right…" Charles says, his voice heavy with regret. His gaze flickers to my trembling hands. I stuff them in my pockets and take a steadying breath.

"I suggest we reconvene at the end of the month and see where we're at."

I frown. "But I'm resigning—"

"Out of the question," Walter butts in. "Take another two weeks to get your head on straight and we'll meet again. In the meantime, I'm writing down a number for you to call."

I pinch the bridge of my nose with my finger

and thumb. "Listen, a shrink isn't going to help—"

"The condition of your sentence is getting therapy. Do you not recall?" Charles cuts in. I avoid his discerning stare while I chew the inside of my cheek. Of course, I remember the day.

The memory is burned in my cranium.

Walter leans forward, giving me a discerning look. "Listen to us, Jack. With the hell you've been through this year, it's no wonder you messed up. And I take responsibility for it. Speak to a therapist. Rest. We'll try again in a couple of weeks. I refuse to give up on you, yet."

I clamp my eyes shut for a moment. Then I force myself to make eye contact with Walter again. This time, he looks less like Voldemort and more like a concerned grandparent. My shame fades just enough to let in the warmth of his care. "Thank you."

Everyone nods at the finality of the moment and Walter hands me a piece of paper. "See you in two weeks."

MY HEART IS HEAVY AS I WALK THE HALLS OF THE hospital. This is a place I called a second home for over a decade. My fellow colleagues go about their duties in a hurry, avoiding eye contact. For the first time, I'm on the other side—like some kind of victim, carrying an awful sickness that's contagious by sight. I imagine they're silently wondering how I can even show my face at work again. After what I did.

I don't blame them.

Working as a heart surgeon in the largest hospital in New York used to be a dream job for me. For a time, it was even everything I hoped it to be.

Long hours. Saving lives. Learning to sleep on my feet. I enjoyed the rush of taking on a lost cause and performing a miracle. Bringing someone back from within an inch of death never got old. And the high afterward? It's like nothing on Earth. It would take hours for me to finally fall asleep when I got home.

I took part in trials, testing new technology that promised to transform heart surgery as we know it. When patients were told nothing could be done, they came to me.

I had twelve years, eight months, and sixteen

days of zero fatalities. A record. I received awards for it.

People called me the heart-saver.

And then in one day, just like that… Everything changed.

I got cocky. Too confident. I was working longer hours than ever. But it wasn't the sleep deprivation that made me lose my streak. It was *her*.

My phone rings, yanking me out of my spiral. I pull it out of my pocket as I reach my car and sigh at the familiar name on the screen.

Speak of the devil.

Beverly. Aka the Ex-Wife. She's the very reason I'm in this mess to begin with.

"What do you want?" I ask, too tired and tense to hide my disdain.

"I need you to take Brodie for a couple of weeks."

Her words land on me like a thunderclap. I climb into my Porsche before the dizziness makes me fall.

My first thought is, *who's dying?* and for one second, I actually hope it's her. There can't be any other reason to call out of the blue and ask me to take our son, when she dragged me through the courts to prevent me from having custody.

My hands grow numb on the steering wheel.

"I thought I was an unfit father who should be limited to only supervised visits?" I say, imitating her lawyer at our last court hearing.

"Don't be like that. My dad needs me to stay with him while he recovers from hip replacement surgery."

I can tell by the tone of her voice that she's not happy about this call. She's probably asked everyone in her circle, even the elderly neighbor, before finally admitting defeat and coming to me.

"Will you take him? My flight leaves in two hours, so you'll have to collect him from kinder-garten," Beverly says, her voice high pitched now.

For the first time all day, my spirits are high enough to bring the corners of my mouth up slightly. Spending time with my boy will give me a sense of purpose and distract me from waiting for the next hospital meeting. I begin to thank my lucky stars.

"Of course. Send my regards to Leo."

"Don't be sarcastic, Jack. Hip surgery isn't without its risks, you know?"

"I'm not being sarcastic," I insist. And it's

true. I might disagree with the man on every political, religious, and social matter, but he is still my son's grandfather. If anything were to happen to him, Brodie would be broken.

That kid doesn't need any more heartache in his childhood.

"Do you want me to swing by and pick up his bags?" I ask, trying to sound less depressed. Just in case she changes her mind. Having Brodie is helping me, not her.

Instead of spending each day and night reliving the past, I'll be focused on making the most of my time with Brodie. My boy.

My brain starts to come up with all of the fun things I plan to do with him. Like take him to the arcades after school or go to the zoo. We could even go on a fishing trip.

I start the car and begin to drive, planning to end up at Beverly's apartment downtown. Her voice stops me in my tracks.

"No need. I've dropped them with your neighbor."

I swallow. She can't be referring to the old man next door. He's as deaf as he is stubborn, and he won't answer the door for anyone.

There's the couple on the other side, but

they're always traveling for work. I'm pretty sure they're still in Peru right now.

"Who?" I ask, dreading the answer even as Chessy's face pops into my head. I've managed to avoid the woman since her birthday, and the humiliation is still too fresh to face her again. I was hoping to avoid her until New Year.

"Francesca Scott. She's the new girl next door. She claimed to know you and was more than happy to help."

There's a slight tone of disapproval in Beverly's voice. I can't work out why, but I'm getting the distinct impression that Beverly knows Chessy. I shake the thought away. How can she know Chessy?

"Okay, fine," I say. Now my brain is jumbled with thoughts and concerns over how I'm going to keep Brodie and my neighbor apart.

How much did Beverly tell her?

The cat is out of the bag now, and goodness knows what she thinks. What kind of dad behaves the way I did the other night?

Brodie is a kindergartener. His favorite game is asking a million invasive questions of anyone he sees.

I just hope I can catch Chessy before school

pick up to give her the low-down on the situation and strict instructions not to mention what happened between us.

Whether it meant anything or not—and it didn't, it was just a drunken fumble, nothing more —the last thing I need my son to know is that I've so much as looked at a woman other than his mother.

I chew my tongue as I enter the apartment complex and take the steps two at a time. When I reach my floor, I swallow the tension in me, then rap my knuckles on Chessy's door.

"She's out."

I turn sharply. It's my neighbor—the grumpy one who never comes out of his apartment other than to trudge to the trash shoot with a black bag.

It seems he's wearing nothing but a thin, blue bathrobe fastened at the waist. All I can see is a pair of veiny legs and bare toes covered in fuzzy white hair. To top it all off, there's tuft of white chest hair peeking out of his bathrobe.

I frown for a moment, thinking that this man can surely not know of Chessy's existence, let alone her whereabouts. He responds with a steely glare framed in white bushy brows. "You stay away from that nice girl. She's out of your league, you know?"

I open and close my mouth several times, lost for words.

What the heck does *that* mean?

Did he somehow hear us through the walls of the apartment? I know we got a little excited in our make out session—my arm bumped the counter a few times and Chessy's knees may have collided with a stool.

For some inexplicable reason, I want to explain the situation. That he's got it all wrong... But maybe that's not entirely true. My thoughts are like scrabble pieces, and I'm struggling to form a coherent thought. A question pops up in my head.

Why does he think I should stay away?

"How do you know her?" I blurt.

The old man bristles at the question and suddenly clutches his robe at his chest, covering himself up. "None of your dang business. You listen to me, she's a sweet vulnerable girl. And I may be old, but I've got a stick."

He staggers toward me, squinting now. Anger radiates off him like steam and his breaths come out in puffs, filling the space between us with the stench of cigarette smoke. "I heard you two the other night…" he mutters, his voice dripping with disdain.

I guess he's not as deaf as I originally thought.

The man thinks we had a drunken one-night stand and I'm the type to use a woman until I'm bored and move onto the next one.

I think about making an explanation. But the man's cold stare tells me I could say one plus one equals two and he wouldn't believe me.

I hold my breath and give him a nod to show I understand. When the man retreats into his cave with a door slam, I scratch the back of my neck and look around the empty hall as if I'll magically find Brodie's bags.

No such luck, so I trudge into my apartment and prepare the guest room.

5

CHESSY

When my door buzzer woke me this morning, the last person I expected to see behind my door was my boss.

Principal Hart.

The kids call her Dragon Lady, and half of the staff picked it up as well.

She struts with her bony shoulders pulled back, puffing out her flat chest and flaring her nostrils, as though she'll let out a blast of fire at any moment.

When she's in a bad mood, she can lower the temperature of a room just by entering it.

It's like she's studied every villain in Roald Dahl's books and taken tips.

Not that she has the looks to fit a Miss Trunchbull character, or anything like that. On the contrary, the woman has sun-kissed blonde hair, wears bold colors, and has the biggest smile in the school.

The thing is, her smile never reaches her eyes.

I get it… Being the principal of a prestigious elementary school is stressful. She wants to be respected.

Maybe even feared.

And it's all about keeping control. I know how the game goes. But when I saw her bulging, pug-like eyes and super fake grin outside my door, I nearly fell over in shock.

"My son is staying with his dad for a while. He —his dad, not my son—lives across the hall, but he's out." My stomach lurched as I followed her line of sight. "Do you mind holding these bags?" she asked in a sickly-sweet voice.

"Are you talking about Jack?" I asked, my arms going numb.

Principal Hart's smile evaporated, and a suspicious look replaced it instead. "Oh. You know my ex-husband?"

Her tone was accusatory.

I prayed to all the gods I could think of,

including the planets, stars, and the whole universe, that she couldn't read my mind. Because I'd started to play a flashback in my head that sent blood to my cheeks. This one was the exact moment Jack's broad hands gripped my thighs. The image brought back the feeling of his stubble grazing my neck. I couldn't help the shiver that ran through my body.

"Only in passing," I said, pushing the image out of my head and hoping my flaming cheeks weren't giving anything away. "I just moved in."

Now I'm in my classroom, clicking my pen and staring out at the sea of kids in front of me. The dull ache of my thumb is barely registering.

Their faces blur as I lose myself in thought.

What did I learn today?

Jack is a dad.

Oh, be still my beating ovaries!

Why, oh why, and just *how* does that revelation instantly move him up the hotness scale?

I mean. I already had a crush on the guy. But now I know he's fathered a son, I'm even more attracted to him.

It must be biology. He's an alpha-dad. A protector.

I roll my bottom lip inward and bite down as I think about having his babies.

One little detail puts a complete downer on everything, though.

His ex-wife is my boss. I groan.

She is the most terrifying woman in the world. And if she finds out what we did the other night… I'm sure I'll lose my job.

My first resolution in my 30s was to go on a health-kick and stop drinking alcohol. I've been chugging water from my giant bottle all day, but all it's done is made me take more bathroom breaks. My head is still sore from my birthday binge.

I sit with my knees crossed, clutching my pencil and staring at the clock over the door. Chair legs scrape across the floor making a jarring sound like nails on a chalkboard.

I take steady breaths and chant in my head.

I love my job. I love my job. I love my job.

The kids scramble with their arms and legs flailing.

"Everyone grab an apron, we're finger painting!" I announce from my desk, wondering when I can make another trip to the bathroom.

The children are gleeful; nothing gives them more joy than making a huge mess.

This is usually my favorite part of the day. When the kids settle down at their desks, armored up with their oversized aprons, I like to listen in and chuckle at all of their little conversations.

Today, though, my thoughts keep oscillating between forbidden fantasies about my hot, single dad neighbor and horror scenarios of getting fired by his ex-wife.

Pieces of one conversation drag me out of my own head long enough to pay attention. A group of toddlers to my right is sharing theories about how Santa Claus can afford to pay all of his elves and deliver on Christmas.

"I think he has a dancing club," Noah says, his shiny blue eyes fixated on his bowl of blue paint as he smashes his hands into it with satisfaction.

Jenkins, a boy beside him with wiry black hair, guffaws. "Dancing club?" he repeats, tickled by the idea. "If Santa dances all year, why is his belly so big?"

Noah rolls his eyes with a big huff and shoots Jenkins a look like he's a thing under a rock.

"*He* doesn't dance," Noah declares. "His woman friends do."

That sets off little alarm bells in my head. My bladder is throbbing as I scramble to my feet and march over to the table, but by the time I get there, it's too late.

Jenkins has slapped his own forehead, forgetting that his palm is covered in paint. A big yellow handprint is now center stage on his face.

"What you talking about, fool? Santa don't have woman friends, and what kind of dancing club are you meaning anyway?"

Noah pauses mid-squelch to sigh. His little shoulders rise and fall.

"It's the North Pole, duh. Obviously, there'll be loads of giant candy canes everywhere and the women will be dancing…"

"Jenkins!" I cut in quickly. My voice is a higher pitch than usual. The two boys look up at me with eyes like saucers. It takes all of my resolve not to burst out laughing—and inevitably pee my pants—as the vision of Santa's pole dancing club takes hold in my mind.

I can't wait to tell my sisters about this later. They love the weird and crazy things I hear these kids talk about in class.

I keep my face neutral. "You've got paint all over your face, sweetie. Let's go clean you up."

I seize the opportunity for a potty break once the kid is paint-free again, but when I return to the classroom, my mouth drops open with horror.

In all of my daydreaming, I guess I lost track of time, because the bell rings just as I step through the door. It's the end of the school day. The kids squeal with joy, wiping their hands on their aprons, the tables... Their legs. Before I can react, every square inch of the room is covered in primary colors.

"Wait a minute!" I yell, raising my palms. "Everyone go wash your hands! And don't touch anything."

There's suddenly a giant slapping sound and then a collective gasp. I whip around, wondering why my butt stings.

My eyes land on the shortest kid in the class, looking up at me with a butter-wouldn't-melt kind of smile. It's also the one kid I've been trying to avoid all day. He has a mop of dark hair over his ears and forehead and a strong resemblance to his dad now that I know what to look for.

I place my hands on my hips.

"Brodie, did you just...?" I trail off. His little hands are clutched together and covered in paint. His smile is wide and innocent, and his teeth gleam at me as his face morphs into a wicked grin.

I arch my back and crane my neck to look. Sure enough, there's a little red handprint on my butt.

There's a stunned silence as everyone looks on, probably wondering what terrible punishment is in store for Brodie.

But he's the principal's son. The kid could likely get away with murder.

A flood of people rushes past my classroom door and I'm reminded that it's home time. Some parents will be wandering in soon, confused as to why I'm not sending their kids out.

I focus on the task at hand; clean up the kids, let them go home, then do damage control.

"Brodie, stay here. I want to speak with you," I say, stopping the kid from following the line out the door.

Before long, it's just the two of us. I opt to have him help me wash down the tables. He seems to enjoy his punishment far too much; rigorously swiping a soggy sponge over the paint and mopping up the residue with a rag. Minutes roll by as we work together in silence, and no one shows up.

I frown at the clock. "Brodie, your dad is coming to pick you up, right?" I ask the little boy.

His gaze moves to the classroom door, expectant, but when no one opens it, he looks back at me and shrugs.

I reason I can take the kid to the principal's office just as soon as I clean myself up. The vice principal will know who to call. Jack must have gotten held up at work or something. I'm just in the middle of rubbing the back of my pants with a wet towel when the door opens.

"So sorry I got held up, I—"

I look up at the sound of that voice. Brodie and I ask, "What are you doing here?" in unison.

Jack is standing in the open doorway, looking flushed. He lowers his eyes to my hand still in its position on my butt. Heat rises to my face. I drop the towel like it's made of lava and clear my throat.

But before I can think of anything to say, Brodie dashes over to Jack and hugs him round the middle. Jack's attention is on Brodie now, and he goes down on one knee to cradle the boy with his eyes shut. "Hey buddy," he says, softly.

"Where's Mom?" Brodie asks when they break apart. The moment seems too sacred for a third wheel, but I'm frozen to the spot for some reason.

Jack tucks his boy's hair behind an ear and gives him a smile. "Your mom needs to help Grandpa for a couple of weeks, so you get to stay with me!"

"Really?" Brodie's face lights up like a Christmas tree and he throws his arms around Jack's shoulders.

I clear my throat again, wishing I could find my voice. Jack looks up at me like he forgot about my existence.

"My ex-wife said she left some bags…"

"Oh. Yes," I say. The school principal's face flashes across my mind. "They're back at my place."

Brodie looks from his dad to me, then back to his dad again. I can see the little cogs moving in his mind.

"Dad, is Miss Scott your new girlfriend?"

Jack balks at the question, and I feel my eyes bulge in their sockets. We both break into a nervous laugh, but then I get a memory flash in my mind's eye: I'm back in Jack's apartment, sitting in his warm lap. His hands are squeezing my thighs as I taste his lips.

I shake the image away, but my cheeks are already burning. I'll bet they're as red as the handprint on my pants.

"Miss Scott is my neighbor," Jack corrects. I marvel at how impassive he looks. I swear the man can walk around a building on fire and not even break into a sweat.

"Dad," Brodie grabs Jack's coat and gives it an urgent tug. "Ask Miss Scott if she wants a ride."

This time, I catch a glimpse of the red tinge in his complexion.

Alright then, I take back my last statement.

Apparently, he picked up on the double meaning too because he turns to me and just opens and closes his mouth soundlessly while Brodie looks on—innocent, expectant, and totally oblivious as to why his dad is struggling to ask the question.

"It's fine," I say, putting Jack out of his misery. I pull out my subway pass from my pocket. "I'll bring the bags over in an hour when I get back."

"An hour?" Brodie's cheery face falls. His reaction sparks something in Jack that makes him look at me with pinched brows.

"I thought you drive to work."

I'm taken aback by his accusatory tone. "I'm out of gas."

"Why don't you fill it up?"

"I'm waiting for payday."

"You can't afford to buy *gas*?" Jack looks at me alarmed. His face has gone pale now. Like the idea that someone could be unable to fill up their car is the most horrifying thought in the world.

The truth is it happens to me most months.

"It's fine," I tell him, almost more concerned for his alarm than I am for myself and my empty bank account. "I've got a pass and I like taking the subway."

It's not totally true. I mean, yes, I can take the subway, but I don't *like* taking it. Half the time, there are no seats except for the odd sticky one that no one would dare sit on. So I have to hold onto something and try not to fall into anyone as the train jostles along the tracks. More often than not, I end up with my face buried in a man's sweaty armpit.

But Jack can't ever know any of that.

He hums in thought while Brodie's head twists side to side—from me to his dad, then back to me again.

"My dad's got a big car, Miss Scott. You'll like

it because it's super clean. My mom says it's like that because he spends more time and money on his car than any—"

"*Okay*, Brodie," Jack butts in, his face reddening fully now. He places a hand over his heart. "I insist you come with us," he says to me.

I'm touched by his sincerity. I take in a deep breath. "It's really nice of you to think of me—"

"Oh no," Jack cuts in, shaking his head violently. "I'm thinking of Brodie. The sooner we get those bags, the sooner we can set up his room."

I swallow my pride and resist the urge to frown. "Let me grab my bag."

Traffic is slow as we crawl across the city and my heartbeat echoes in my head as I try not to listen to Brodie and Chessy playing twenty questions.

I'm gripping the steering wheel so hard, the whites of my knuckles are on show. The conversation soon pivots to me. "My dad is the smartest person I know, Miss Scott."

"Oh, really?" she replies, her pitch too high to sound normal. I can feel the heat of her inquisitive gaze on me. "Why do you say that?"

Brodie doesn't hesitate. "Because he knows how to bring people back from the dead," he says proudly.

Chessy gasps. "You're a doctor?" she asks me.

Brodie replies before I can unstick my lips and respond.

"He's a surgeon, Miss. I heard him telling my mom that he held a man's heart in his hands when the man died. And then he fixed it, and the dead man came back to life."

"Wow, that's amazing," Chessy replies, and for a moment my chest swells.

But Brodie isn't done.

"My mom says Dad is just as good at breaking hearts too…"

A prickle of annoyance claws up my arms and two invisible hands clutch my throat. I wonder what other poisonous thoughts my wife has imbedded in our son's impressionable mind.

"We're here!" I announce, signaling the end of that conversation. We pull into the underground parking lot and Brodie rolls his window down. "Hello, hello!" he shouts with his head sticking out, listening with glee to his voice echoing in the dark garage.

"Dad, can Miss Scott come over for dinner?" he asks the entire garage.

I love my son, and I feel blessed that I finally get to spend some unsupervised time with him.

But I swear, if he keeps this up, the next two weeks are going to be the end of me.

Thankfully, Chessy is quick to shoot down the idea. "Oh no, love. I've got plans tonight. But thanks for thinking of me," she says. Her voice is melodic and soft. It does something funny to my stomach. I can't work out if it's a good feeling or a bad one.

Then again, I haven't fully processed the fact that she's been my son's kindergarten teacher all this time, and I didn't know.

How could my own son's teacher be living next door for months without me realizing? What kind of father does that make me?

Beverly has a lot to answer for. If her lawyers hadn't painted me as a disgraced surgeon, barely capable of taking care of myself, let alone a kid, I'd have had more contact. I would have been there for his first day at school and at pickup.

But Beverly was adamant that I keep my distance. That visits could only be in public places, and she needed to be there too. How could I have known? The fact that she now drops our son in my hands for two weeks without so much as batting an eyelid just validates my suspicions. Keeping Brodie away from me was never about keeping him safe. It was about control and hurting me.

"Okay," Brodie looks down in defeat. It takes a few seconds for me to remember what we were talking about. *Oh, yes.* Brodie wants Chessy to come over for dinner. That would have been incredibly awkward for us. Not that Brodie knows, or needs to.

Then he's struck by another thought and turns hopeful while I'm parked in our spot. "How about tomorrow night?"

I smile to myself. Kids are experts at over-coming obstacles. They truly make excellent sales-people. It's just as well that child labor is illegal in this country. If big corporations had kinder-garteners knocking on doors to sell their products, most households would run into bankruptcy by Thanksgiving.

I realize Brodie will not stop. I need to step in and save Chessy from being interrogated until she caves in and agrees to do whatever my son wants. Before I can, though, she raises her head and gives Brodie a reply.

"That's very sweet of you to offer, Brodie, but I'll see you in class every day and you and your dad have a lot of fun plans that do not involve me."

Her tone is so final and authoritative that I'm reminded she knows how to handle an excitable child. It's her job after all, and I was a fool to forget it.

Brodie falls silent. I can see that her words have planted a seed of thought in his mind. I watch it grow as we walk up to the elevator, like a weed sped up in real time. "What are we going to do, Dad?" His voice is laced with excitement.

I resist the urge to glare at Chessy. Now Brodie will be expecting us to do big and exciting things every day after school.

It's not that I don't want to take my son out and have fun with him, I just don't like making any promises—a habit anyone who's ever worked in a hospital is likely to adopt. Too often, I'll be sitting down to eat when a call out of the blue will summon me back in to work. Or my pager will buzz right in the middle of a movie.

Even when I'm not on call, if there's a horrid accident and the on-call surgeon is sick, I'll have to go in.

I'm a much bigger fan of being spontaneous —less pressure and less disappointment.

But I remind myself that I don't need to worry about it anymore. I'm on a sabbatical. No one is calling me to go in and cut someone open.

In any case, I've not planned out the next couple of weeks. So, I opt for the ominous yet thrilling answer that will pacify any kid. "It's a surprise."

Chessy opens her door and pulls two blue luggage bags out into the hall. "Here you go."

Our fingers brush as I take a bag from her, and my eyes meet hers for the first time since we were at the school. I see tiny flecks of gold in her pupils and her long lashes flutter. Everything zings.

I clench my jaw, trying to ignore the sensations rolling through my body, and pick up the other bag too. "Say goodbye to Miss Scott," I say to Brodie as he zooms around the hall, pretending to be a plane. He promptly stops in his tracks, turns to Chessy, and lifts a solemn hand in the air. "Bye."

With one final nod to Chessy, I turn and unlock the door to my apartment. But just as I open it, I catch a figure in my peripheral vision. It's the old man in his blue robe. His eyes are slits as he stares at me. He doesn't need to say it, I can practically hear his thought echoing in my mind, warning me to stay away from Chessy.

"Where's Mom?" Brodie asks as I close the door. I resist the frown tugging on my mouth and force a smile instead.

"I told you. She's with Grandpa, bud."

"For how long?"

I resist the urge to grab a strong drink and go to the fridge instead. "Two weeks."

I hand him a bottle of water and take one for myself. His expression has turned serious.

"That's fourteen days," he declares, looking down at the floor in concentration. "Because a week is seven days and seven plus seven is fourteen," he continues.

"That's right," I say. After I've emptied the bottle, I carry his bags to his room. His little footsteps follow mine. Just before the doorway, he barrels through the open door and launches himself on the bed.

"Is this where I'm gonna sleep?" he asks, yanking off his shoes. Before I can tell him not to, he starts jumping on the mattress.

His face is flushed when he finally flops backs on the bed, and I don't have it in me to tell him off. I begin to unpack his things and he launches into another round of quick-fire questions.

"Is Grandpa going to die?"

"No."

"Can we go visit him?"

"No."

"Why not?"

"Because he lives eight hours away and you've got school in the morning."

"Do you like my teacher? Miss Scott?"

I pause, holding a pair of his shorts mid-air. Before I can think of a reasonable response, Brodie starts talking at full speed.

"She's real nice, Dad. And smart too. Did you know she can say the alphabet backwards? And she knows about all of the presidents of the United States."

I smile to myself and carry on putting Brodie's clothes away. "Cool."

There's a thump, and Brodie's little face suddenly pops into view from over my shoulder. "Dad. Can we have pizza tonight? Mom never lets me eat pizza."

My smile slips at the mention of my ex-wife again. "She doesn't let you eat pizza?" I ask him, turning to look him in the eye. His mouth drops, forming a perfect o. "Yeah. She says it's bad for me and even worse for her hips."

I resist the urge to make a sarcastic remark and just pat him on the shoulder instead. Then I remember it's been weeks since I've been to the store, and I've not got much food in. I haven't even noticed until now because I've barely been eating. I pinch the bridge of my nose for a second, feeling a headache coming on.

Going out for pizza isn't a bad idea.

"What's your favorite? Pepperoni?" I ask, shutting the drawer and zipping up the luggage bags. Brodie's face twists in revulsion. "No way, Dad. I like BBQ. You know, with the little sausage slices on it?"

My chest tightens. "Since when did you stop liking pepperoni? It used to be all you ate."

Brodie shrugs. No big deal. My chest tightens. How much do I not know?

How is it that my son's pizza preference changed, and I didn't know about it?

"If your mom won't let you eat pizza, how do you…?" Brodie's devilish grin stops me mid-sentence.

"Noah's birthday party… He had BBQ pizza, and I ate three whole slices."

He stuffs a hand over his mouth to stifle a delighted chuckle, but my heart sinks.

Eating pizza shouldn't be a crime.

I curl my fingers into a tight fist and clench my jaw as I make a mental note to talk to Beverly about restricting our son from basic childhood treats.

When we were married, we even had pizza night during the week. Wednesdays… That was the two-for-one day at our local establishment.

I grind my teeth but force a smile despite it, determined to hide my irritation from my son. Whatever ill feeling I have toward my ex-wife, I don't want Brodie to grow up thinking I hate her. At this present moment, though, I'm pretty certain that I do.

"Go put your shoes back on," I tell him. "We're going out."

7

CHESSY

I sit on my bed cross-legged and chew my bottom lip, listening to the number on the other end ring.

"Come on… Pick up…" I mutter to myself.

The situation has escalated to the point where I need back up. And I don't care what's going on with either of my sisters. This is an emergency.

When they're both finally on the group call, my racing heart begins to slow. Just the sound of their voices has a soothing effect on me.

"What's wrong?" Leila asks, her tone dipping when I try and fail to sound bright and breezy.

"Why do you say that? I'm fine… Crazy weather we're having, isn't it? It's warm one second, then freezing cold the next. Anyone would think we're in London, am I right?" I ramble.

Lucy huffs. I know it's her, because she always huffs when someone starts to make small talk. Lucy thinks it's just a waste of time.

"Just tell us what the drama is," she says, too blunt for my liking. But that's Lucy's style. She doesn't sugar-coat her thoughts. Leila is far more diplomatic.

This is exactly why I need to speak to them both about Jack. I need the combination of Lucy's straight-talk and Leila's compassion to navigate this conversation.

I take a breath.

"Do you both remember when Wyatt proposed?"

My sisters say, "Yeah," in unison. To my surprise, no one starts gushing about it. Then I remember that's my thing. I clear my throat, slightly embarrassed at my own corniness.

"Well, remember that rude neighbor who told us to be quiet?"

There's a groan, and I'm not sure who it came from. Then Lucy speaks and I realize that was her.

"You're not dating him, are you?" she asks.

When I don't answer immediately, my sisters groan in unison. The sound prickles me, and just like that, my heart rate is picking up again. "No," I say, finally. But I'm far too late to sound convincing.

"What's going on, then?" Leila asks doubtfully.

I take a steadying breath and launch into the story, leaving out some of the important details. Like what happened on the night of my birthday, the fact his son is in my class, and that his ex-wife is my boss.

My sisters listen in silence. To my relief, no one groans again. But of course, as soon as I reach the scandalous parts, their moans will no doubt rise like a symphony.

"...and you know I've always had a thing for grumpy, single dads..." I say, trailing off.

"Hmm. Sounds like he comes with a lot of emotional baggage. Are you sure you want to unpack all of that?" Leila asks.

I put the phone on speaker and lay back on the bed, staring up at the ceiling as Jack's face flashes into my mind's eye. I can still feel the heat of his hands on my hips. The memory-taste of his lips transports me to a campfire by the lake.

Lucy scoffs. "This is our Chessy, remember? She'll see him as a wounded baby bird and want to fix him."

She's not wrong. I'm a sucker for a hot guy with a tortured past. But it's that kind of attraction that has gotten me into some very bad breakups. I'm thirty now, and I promised myself I'd stop falling into those situations. I shake my head. "I can't."

There's a stunned silence, then a cough, and I picture Leila choking on her own spit at my uncharacteristic response.

"So... You're *not* dating the guy?"

I bite my lip for a second. "Not dating... No. But on my birthday, I had a little too much to drink and—"

My sisters gasp in perfect unison. "You slept with him!"

I frown. "No. I didn't, actually."

I'm sure my sisters think I've jumped right into bed with every guy I ever swooned over. But I have morals. Little do they know I've never actually let a man stay the night. I've never even been with the same guy long enough to get past second base. I've always wanted to wait until I found Mr. Right.

I keep thinking I've found him, but he always ends up being Mr. Wrong.

"Then what is it? Why are you talking to us about it?" Lucy asks, her frustration growing audibly. Lucy hates it when I tiptoe around a topic.

Knowing they can't help me without the full story, I try to fill in the blanks.

"We made out and now I can't stop thinking about him."

"Of course," Leila says, mostly to herself I reckon. I can almost see her lifting a hand in exasperation. Neither of them says it, but I know what my sisters are thinking; *There she goes again.* Falling head over heels for another guy.

"Are you asking for our opinion?" Lucy asks, sounding confused. I get why, because I don't ever ask for their opinion on whether to date a guy or not. In the past, I've always jumped right in with two feet. But this time, things are... Complicated.

"He's off-limits," I say, thinking about Brodie.

"Oh no. Don't tell me he's not single, Chessy," Leila says. Her voice is a hallowed whisper, as though the very words might summon the love police to come take me away.

I've been in some bad relationships, but I've

never dated a guy who was not single. At least... I don't *think* I have.

"He's divorced. It's not that. It's just..." For some reason, the words keep getting tangled around my tongue. I'm struggling to spit them out. I shut my eyes and throw my hands over my face.

"Chessy?" Lucy calls out. "Did she leave the call?" Lucy asks Leila.

"I don't think so..." Leila replies. "Chessy, do you want to come over? Blaze can swing by and pick you up."

I roll onto my stomach and bury my face in my pillow.

On the one hand, it would be good to get out of this lonely apartment and put as much distance between me and my hot neighbor as possible. But on the other hand, my head is thumping, and I just want to hide under the covers and pretend I don't exist.

"Thanks, but I think I'm going to have an early night."

"Wait," Lucy says, before I can end the call. "Is that it? How can you leave us hanging?"

"Exactly," Leila says. "You're telling us you like the guy, and it sounds like he's at least attracted to you too… He's not in a relationship, but you say he's off limits…"

I've told them just enough to pique their interest, but not enough to stop them from obsessively picking through my words for clues and painting their own theory on what's going on.

I can't hide under my covers after all.

I summon all my strength and shut my eyes again. Then I blurt it out in one breath.

"I'm his son's kindergarten teacher and the kid's mom is the principal."

The words hang in the air and vibrate around the room.

Several moments pass by in silence while I wait for someone to speak. I can just picture my sisters both staring at me, blinking.

It's Lucy who finally breaks the silence.

"*What* the actual *heck.*"

I roll my lips inward and bite down while Leila and Lucy launch into a conversation with each other, as if I'm not here.

"Isn't there some kind of law against making out with a parent?"

"The principal is the ex-wife? Even if it's allowed, she's not going to be happy when she finds out her son's kindergarten teacher has been sucking face with her…"

"It's not like that," I insist, my face growing hot. "You're making it sound more scandalous than it is."

My sisters fall silent for a moment. Then Leila talks to me like I'm a kid who just got caught painting naughty pictures on the bathroom wall.

"Chessy. You can't go after this guy. You'll end up broken-hearted and worse—you'll lose your job."

"I know. I know," I say, pulling my knees up to my chin. "But now his kid is staying with him for the next couple of weeks, and I don't know how I'm supposed to just pretend—"

"You have to," Lucy cuts in, her voice firm. "Chessy. You are absolutely right; Jack is *off-limits*. There's way too much drama there, and I know it's hard, but you're gonna have to be professional."

"You've got too much to lose," Leila adds.

Their words weigh heavy on my mind, but a part of me isn't surprised. I expected this kind of reaction, but I can't deny a tiny part of me was hoping they'd tell me something different. Something like, *'Who cares about the consequences? Follow your heart.'*

Or *'You're not doing anything wrong. Love conquers all.'*

That would be *my* advice if this was happening to them. But it's happening to me, and my sisters are far too sensible to be telling me to hop into a relationship with Jack.

"Blaze will come pick you up tomorrow. You're coming over for dinner," Leila says. The finality in her voice tells me it's useless to argue. "We're going to get a hot meal into you and talk everything through. Besides… I need your opinion on bachelorette party ideas."

"If the party doesn't involve the three of us in my game room, with virtual reality headsets and a mountain of donuts, I don't want it," Lucy declares, sounding far too serious.

Besides from her love of cosplay, Lucy is a huge gamer and introvert—even more so since she met Wyatt. Before meeting him, she would come out shopping or go to a club. Now all she wants to do is hide in her Bat Cave or go hiking in the middle of nowhere.

I sigh, looking around my dark empty room with sadness.

It's easy for my sisters to tell me to do the right thing and avoid Jack. They're in happy relationships.

I would give anything to have a doting man in my bed right now, warming it up for me and wrapping me up in his big strong arms.

My brain conjures up the image, and of course, it's Jack's face on the imaginary man's body.

"I've gotta go, the tour is leaving in ten minutes," Lucy says.

My fantasy shatters.

"I know I'm probably wasting my breath here, but, Chessy… Behave yourself. Please. Any relationship with this neighbor is forbidden, you got it?"

"Don't say that!" Leila says with a gasp. "Now you've gone and made him even more tempting by calling him the forbidden fruit. I remember when I thought I wasn't allowed to be with Blaze. He became ten times hotter."

I snort.

She's not wrong, but it amuses me that my sisters keep talking to each other like I'm not on the call. It's the curse of being the baby.

"Don't worry. I'm not going to jump on him

just because you say it's forbidden," I mumble. Their responding sounds of disapproval tell me my words did nothing to ease their worries. I tilt my head back and think about changing the topic. It'll have to be a juicy one to be a successful distraction.

I rack my brain and it lands on the one topic that never fails to elicit strong emotions. One or both of my sisters always launch into a big, angry rant.

"Lucy, before you go, are you inviting Mom to the wedding?"

There's a gasp, and I think it came from Leila. It's Lucy who replies in a curt voice.

"No. She didn't come to Leila's wedding, why should I bother inviting her to mine?"

"Mom was having surgery; it wasn't her fault!" Leila argues.

Our mom is always a testy topic, but I'm relieved I'm no longer getting lectured about Jack.

"I think she could have rescheduled it to some date *after* your wedding if it was that important to her, Leila," Lucy snaps. "I mean, liposuction can wait a week or two, don't you think?"

There's a hurt silence.

I can hear Leila's heavy breaths and my

stomach lurches with regret. Maybe switching the topic to our estranged mom, who seems to care a lot more about her new family than any of us, was not a good idea after all.

"Forget it, okay?" It's a vain attempt to make my sisters magically forget all about this phone call. "Have fun on your tour, Lucy. Leila, I'll see you tomorrow night."

I still have a fake smile on my face when I end the call, but I finally let it fall as a heaviness spreads throughout my chest. My stomach is hollow, and I roll onto my side in a ball. Hollywood movies make single life look so glamorous. Part of me wants to write a letter of complaint to somebody. We're all being lied to.

I summon my inner Beyoncé and tell myself I'm a strong, independent woman making it in the Big Apple. People *dream* of living my life. I'm free to party when I want, I have complete autonomy over what I do with my time, my body, my money.

It works for a nanosecond, then I'm deflated again.

The truth is… my single life is so freaking lonely.

My sisters are my best friends, and they're

both off the market—completely disinterested in doing anything remotely fun.

Sure, I can get a guy to keep me company. But can I get one to commit? So far, it seems easier to tame a feral cat than to get a man to settle down with me.

Maybe I'm drawn to Jack because he's the only man I've seen every day without fail, living right across the hall. That makes him my constant. He's got a kid, so I'm assuming he's responsible and caring. And there's the fact that he's such an amazing kisser—the best of all the guys I've ever kissed. I want to kiss him again. Sober this time, so I can really enjoy it.

Too bad I'll lose my job and any possibility of getting another one if I do anything with him. Sure, we could try and keep it a secret, but as soon as my principal discovers our relationship, she'll fire me on the spot and have me blacklisted. Then I'll be evicted because I won't be able to get another teaching job and I won't have any money to pay rent. I'll finally have to move in with Leila and Blaze, the love birds.

But maybe I won't need a job if I end up with Jack? After all, my sisters always joke I was born in the wrong decade. Being a 1950s wife doesn't sound so bad to me. He'll go to work all day while I doll myself up, take care of our beautiful mansion, and teach our half-dozen kids at home.

I sigh, dreaming of a picture-perfect family life with Jack.

Maybe the two of us can make things work. I could be Brodie's stepmom! Not an evil one, like in the movies. I'd be the best stepmom ever. We'd go out on big adventures together—road trip across the states.

We'll camp and lay on the grass, gazing up at the night sky while I tell him all about the constellations and the stories behind each one. Jack will caress my hand as he lays on the other side of me and press his lips on my arm while I talk.

I jump up out of bed and reprimand myself. The vision fades. I can't be thinking about Jack this way. It's the loneliness guiding my over-active imagination.

I don't have feelings for Jack. I barely know the guy. Besides, I *can't* do anything now that I know he's Brodie's dad. I curl my hands into fists and march to my bathroom.

"Get a *grip*, Chessy," I say into the mirror, clutching the sides of the sink. I puff out my cheeks, then I head for the shower, promising myself I'll keep my head down and stay out of trouble from now on.

I lose myself in thought as I turn the shower on and get undressed. Then I hatch a master plan.

Once I get paid, I'm going out to a bar to meet someone. Or I'll go to the mall and meet The One as we both reach for a pair of men's pajamas. Just like that old man in The Holiday talks about.

He'll say he just needs the bottoms. I'll say I just need a top.

We'll both know, right there and then—this is meant to be.

I swoon when the jets hit my body and the bathroom fills with steam. My mood is already lifting as my imagination plays out all kinds of romantic scenarios. Then I catch sight of something black in my peripheral vision and my body stiffens.

My eyes dart to the black thing and when my vision focuses, I can just make out the spread of long hairy legs by the shower head.

I swear on my life and the lives of both my sisters that it's the biggest freaking spider I've ever seen. A glass-shattering scream emits from my open mouth, and I stare at the thing in sheer horror.

To my surprise, the arachnid doesn't scurry away, but sits still instead. I bet it's laughing, and that it has a dark, wicked laugh. Its legs are bent slightly, and I'm certain I can see all of its eight eyes, staring me down like a villain in a superhero movie.

I'm frozen. Too scared to move, in case I startle the spider and it makes a run for me.

Lucy likes spiders. She says they can't see very well and don't actually run toward people. If they do, it's by mistake. But my past experiences say the contrary. I've had a spider run to me and launch its little body at my leg. Now tell me how that's not a spider with malicious intent.

I've been around long enough to know that whether they are harmless or not, spiders are little ninjas. They can swoosh across the room like Tarzan, scramble up your leg faster than a cheetah, and eat you for dinner if given half a chance.

Well, not tonight. I'm not giving this monstrosity a chance. Another scream rips out of my mouth like a tormented soul is trapped inside of me.

That's when the room shakes. I can't tell if

I'm experiencing an earthquake or if my scream turned supersonic.

I want to let out another scream, but I don't want to make the building collapse. So, I clamp both hands over my mouth and let out a muffled one instead.

Suddenly, the door flies open with a tremendous bang, prompting the spider to scurry up the tile a few inches. I react to that with a backward hop and a yelp, and swivel to see the door hanging off its hinges at an awkward angle. Then my eyes meet a pair of intense blue ones. They bore into mine with such ferocity, I feel my body flush with heat.

I take in a bare chest and bulging muscles. A pair of thin cotton shorts sits low on trim hips, and I can just see a little tuft of dark hair sticking out from the waistband. The two lines of his hip bones point like arrows to a beautiful bulge covered by the thin material of his shorts.

My eyes slink back up to meet his and that's when I realize I'm naked and I still have my hands on my mouth. I lower them immediately, trying to cover myself up while Jack looks around the bathroom, his biceps flexing.

"Who hurt you?" he growls, and the sound vibrates off the tiled walls.

I'm too stunned to reply with anything other than a shake of my head. I don't have a spare hand to point at the wretched spider that is now climbing up to the ceiling.

Jack follows my line of sight and his shoulders sag. There's a thud and I notice an axe drop by his feet.

Without another word, Jack grabs a towel from the rack and tosses it to me. "Cover up and let me deal with this."

I do as I'm told and wrap the towel around me, edging away from the shower. Jack steps past and our bare arms touch for the briefest moment. It sends a current through me.

I find strength in my legs once more and dash out of the bathroom, wanting to get as far away from the spider as possible.

Jack grumbles something inaudible for several moments, then charges out of the bathroom with his hands cupped. I point to them. "Is it in there?" I ask, in terror.

The thought of the spider's feet touching Jack's palms makes my skin crawl. I almost drop the towel as I leap out of his way.

"It's just a little spider," he says in a low voice as he heads for my bedroom window.

"No, it's not. It is a monster!" I shout at the top of my lungs.

Jack releases the spider into the night and shuts the window. Then he turns to look at me, his face dark in the shadows. The scowl on his face is unmistakable, though.

"How dare you," he growls, taking a few steps toward me. I step back, my arms trembling. "I thought someone was in here. I thought you were being attacked!"

I drop my mouth, shocked by his fury. "Oh! I'm sorry for scaring you, but I had a *freaking* Goliath spider in my shower!" I spit, scowling back now.

Being angry at Jack makes it easier to ignore the other feelings I have toward him.

I mean, there can't be many things more attractive than a shirtless man tearing through my bathroom door to rescue me with an axe. He stands in a cloud of pure masculinity and my entire body is compelled to submit to him. Don't judge me. It's just basic biology.

He takes another step. "You're lucky Brodie is asleep. He would have been terrified." I recoil a little.

Brodie.

Then my stomach knots itself. "I'm… Sorry." The last thing I want to do is scare the kid.

"And thanks," I add. Feeling foolish now.

Jack simply nods and marches out of the room, picking up his axe on his way out. Then he pauses, props the axe against a chair and turns around to face me, his expression softening. "I expect I won't be able to get someone out until morning, but I'll pay for a new door. In the mean-time, you're coming with me."

"Wh-what?" I ask.

Without hesitation, Jack picks me up, and the towel threatens to unravel. I fist the fluffy cotton desperately and cross my legs to keep my modesty, while Jack holds me firm against his chest.

My sisters' warnings flash across my mind while my hot neighbor carries me all the way to his apartment. I get an eyeful of my front door, with a big chuck missing from it.

"I can't stay with you! You know that, right?" I whisper as he carries me to his room—for the second time in a week.

I eye the closed bedroom door in the hall, hoping Brodie is still blissfully asleep.

"It's not safe for you in your place without a front door."

I open and close my mouth soundlessly as I try to make sense of the situation.

"I need clothes... My phone..." I say. I'll give the guy credit for his chivalry, but his plan needs work. Now he's got a wet, naked, kindergarten teacher on his bed, just a few feet away from his sleeping son. So much for him being a deep thinker. There are so many flaws in this plan, I don't think he's thought any of this through.

Jack lowers me onto his bed. When he releases me, a chill takes over my body.

"Just wear one of my shirts, and we'll figure it out in the morning. Besides, it's getting late."

He tosses me a blue shirt, and I'm enveloped in his woody scent as I hold it up to my chest. My defenses lower as I take a big whiff. For a second, I forget myself.

"You know, anyone would think you like having me in your bed," I blurt.

Jack's eyes flash in alarm at my words and he jerks his thumb toward the doorway. "Keep it down, will you?"

I shut my mouth and nod.

I don't even know where that line came from.

I'm so used to flirting with guys, some things just pop out of my mouth without input from my brain.

I nod several times, wondering if I somehow slipped in the shower and bumped my head. Maybe this whole experience is just some kind of fever dream.

If this was a fever dream, though, it's 99% likely that Jack wouldn't plonk me on his bed and leave the room. Which is exactly what he does.

The door clicks shut behind him and I stay frozen, wondering how the heck I'm going to get up and get ready for work in the morning without Brodie seeing me wearing his dad's shirt and getting the wrong idea.

One thing is for sure, with my overactive imagination fed by new images of Jack standing in the doorway to my bathroom, coupled with the stress of avoiding his son, I'm not getting any sleep tonight.

8

JACK

After patching up Chessy's front door with duct tape, I head for my kitchen and pace the room in stress. I am *such* an idiot for bringing her back to my apartment.

My brain can't stop painting a picture of her laying in my bed, right next door to my son. If he so much as gets an inkling that his teacher is in my bedroom, heaven knows what he's going to tell Beverly.

Beverly will freak out, that's for sure.

She might even abandon her dad, come right back home, yank Brodie from my clutches, and make sure I never see him again.

Chessy would be fired.

It would be an utter disaster.

But when I heard Chessy's screams, all I could see was red.

I survey the damage on my elbow from when I smashed the safety glass to grab the axe. Brodie had just gone to sleep, his favorite movie playing on the tablet in his room, when I heard her.

I don't know why my brain immediately conjured up the thought that someone had climbed in through the fire escape and attacked her. Probably because I've done surgery on patients who have been attacked in their homes. This is New York after all. These apartments aren't in the nicest part of the city. And Chessy is all alone. Vulnerable.

My main priority was to get into her apartment at whatever cost and save her from danger. But what I saw when I kicked in her bathroom door was far more disturbing than an intruder.

I saw terror in Chessy's eyes as they landed on me.

I frightened her. Probably more than that stupid spider. If the woman ever went camping and saw an actual Goliath, I think she'd have a heart attack.

I just needed to get Chessy out of danger. But now that her door is compromised, I've made the situation even worse. It didn't feel like I had much of an option at the time; I needed to take her into my room to be able to protect her.

Now she's in my bed, wearing nothing but my shirt, without any of her things.

I don't want to invade her privacy and go into her apartment for her, but it was already a risk taking her to my room in the first place. Brodie could have opened the door at any minute. Next time, I might not be so lucky.

I ruffle my hair and sigh, eyeing the bottle of whiskey on the counter with longing.

Alcohol won't serve me tonight. I shouldn't have it just lying around either, with Brodie staying with me. I pick it up and put it in the glass cabinet with the rest of my bottles. Then I lock the doors, wondering how the heck I'm going to get out of this tricky situation.

My evil brain keeps pulling up the mental snapshot of Chessy standing naked before me. I have goosebumps, and my heart is throbbing painfully in my chest.

At the time, the last thing on my mind was her body. But now that the danger has passed and I'm alone in a dark room, my imagination is going wild.

I'm a red-blooded male. How could I not have some reaction to seeing an incredibly attractive woman in the shower? Even if she happens to be my son's kindergarten teacher and thinking about her without clothes on is highly improper.

I have to admit I'll never be able to look at her the same way.

It's like accidentally discovering a hidden Christmas present, then having to put it back and pretend you didn't see anything.

Worse, Christmas will never come because she is absolutely off-limits.

My gut grows taut.

Before my mind wanders off processing the situation any further, I tiptoe to Brodie's room and open the door a crack to check on him. The hall light settles on his sleeping form and I exhale with relief at the sight.

I shut the door silently and walk back into my kitchen with my shoulders squared.

Now I'm alone and confident there can't be any prying eyes, I begin to pace the room while I go over my options.

Option one makes me lick my bottom lip and bite on it; I could go into my room and ravish Chessy. Stuff her mouth with one of my ties to muffle her screams while I give her the best night of her life. I'd take her in the bedroom, the bathroom, up against the window overlooking the city, and twice on the counter. And I won't stop pleasuring her until she's simmering in post orgasmic bliss, begging me to stop.

I shut my eyes with longing. It's been so long... I haven't been with a woman since Beverly. Just kissing Chessy was like a healing balm, soothing all my wounds.

I shake my head, forcing the indecent thoughts out of my head.

I can't think about her like that. It's wrong.

Option one is most definitely *not* on the cards.

My brain moves on.

Option two; call someone to fix the door at the crack of dawn, then distract Brodie in his room, while Chessy sneaks out.

I nod to myself. It's the best idea I've got.

I pull out my phone.

———

There's a soft knock on the door just before six in the morning. I jerk awake at the sound and roll off the couch with a yawn.

"Thanks for doing this," I say to the handyman when I open my door.

It's the same guy who changed the locks from the other night. "What the heck happened?" he asks, looking at all the duct tape. I pop my head out in the hall and check that the coast is clear, then I look at the replacement door propped up against the wall. "A simple misunderstanding," I mutter. "How long do you think you'll be?"

The handyman shrugs. "Twenty minutes, half an hour tops," he says. I pull a few twenty-dollar bills from my pocket and stuff them in his hand. "Make it fifteen and I'll double it."

"Yes, sir."

I am antsy as the man sets to work, and I hover near Brodie's door, praying to God he doesn't wake up yet. Luckily, my prayers are answered, and he doesn't.

With the new door in place and another set of keys in hand, I tap on my bedroom door and press my ear to it.

No response.

I tap again, harder this time, while keeping a chameleon eye on Brodie's.

A couple of minutes roll by and I start to sweat. All I have to do is get Chessy out of my apartment before Brodie wakes up, and we've got away with this crazy situation.

I turn the handle and push the door open, peering inside.

"Hey," I whisper. "Chessy, are you awake?"

My ears prick up at the sound of the toilet flushing in the master bathroom. The door opens, at the same moment I hear Brodie's door handle turn. "Dad…"

I dash to a stunned Chessy, forcing her back into the bathroom. "Hey bud! I'm just taking a shower," I call out. I shoo Chessy into the bath, switch on the faucet and drag the shower curtain across at the sound of Brodie's approaching footsteps. Luckily, Chessy is hidden by the time my son reaches the bathroom.

"Hi Dad."

I plaster on a beaming smile and turn. "Hey buddy. How did you sleep? Did you have any crazy dreams last night?"

Brodie proceeds to open the cabinets with curiosity, while I hover near the bath, hoping Chessy can keep quiet. This is *not* how I pictured the morning. The room begins to fill with steam, and it brings back memories of last night. Why does the universe keep putting me in a hot steamy bathroom with Chessy?

Brodie eyes me with a frown. "Why have you still got your clothes on, Dad?" he asks, eyeing my shorts. "You don't wear clothes in the shower, silly."

My heart is pounding. "I'm waiting for the water to heat up."

Brodie rocks on the balls of his feet. "Mom says it's a waste of water to let it keep running like that. And she says cold showers are good for you."

I freeze, scrambling to think of what I can possibly do to avoid having to climb into the bath naked... With Chessy. "Well... I..."

Brodie's face lights up. "Can I have a shower, first? I like cold water." He starts to tug on his shirt to pull it over his head and I break into a nervous sweat. "No," I say, grabbing his shirt and yanking it down again. "Why don't you go grab some left-over pizza, while I take a shower? Then you can go in."

Brodie frowns. "But I want to take a shower now. Besides, Mom says pizza isn't breakfast." He starts to make a beeline for the shower.

Frustration takes over me. I drop my shorts and hop in the shower before Brodie can reach it.

"Go grab that pizza, bud. I'll be right out, I promise," I say, leaning around the curtain.

"But Mom says…"

"I'll talk to your mom. Don't you worry about it. Now go on," I say through gritted teeth.

"Okay," Brodie says, skipping out of the bathroom. I turn toward the water spray and sigh with relief. Then my eyes meet with Chessy's and we both jump.

My blue shirt is soaked to her skin. It's an incredible sight.

We stay frozen for a few seconds, in the most awkward situation I've ever been in.

"You know, Brodie's mom is right, pizza isn't breakfast," she says.

I clamp a hand over her mouth and listen out for Brodie. But I can just make out the sound of him banging around in the kitchen. I give Chessy a warning look, then I notice her eyes stretched wide and staring downward.

I cock a brow at her to say, really? Is that necessary? She meets my gaze, and her face reddens.

She's so close to me, it would be easy to steal a kiss. I pull my hand away from her mouth, and water droplets sit on her lips like morning dew.

If the circumstances happened to be less stressful, I think I'd have leaned in and gone for it.

She looks delicious. And she's right within my reach.

But Brodie will be back soon, and I need to figure out how to get Chessy out of my apartment without him knowing about it.

"Wait for me to cough, then wrap yourself up in a towel, take the keys on the bed and make a run for your apartment."

Chessy nods, keeping her mouth shut. But her gaze drops to my manhood again, and this time, her brows rise. I curse my body for giving away just how attracted I am to her. "Focus please," I mutter to her, and she meets my gaze once more.

Her face is flushed with color now.

I cover myself with one hand and lean around Chessy to turn off the water with the other. Then I press my finger to my lips before climbing out of the tub.

"Okay, bud. I've got a big question for you," I say, after wrapping a towel around my waist and walking into the kitchen. Brodie looks up from his plate of food with excitement.

"What is it, Dad?"

I gesture to his room. "Come on."

Brodie jumps down from the stool by the counter and runs into his room at full speed. I follow him inside and make a loud cough. Then I shut the door.

"What do you want to do after school today?" I say as loud as I can, hoping Chessy's footsteps can't be heard from Brodie's room. So far, all seems to be silent.

Brodie gasps. "Can we go to the zoo and see the penguins? I love penguins."

"Sure, sure," I say, nodding. I glance at the door, wondering how long Chessy will need to get away. "And tomorrow? What do you want to do tomorrow?"

"Can we go to Miss Scott's place for dinner? I've never been inside her apartment."

My blood turns cold at the mention of Chessy's name. But then I'm reminded she's Brodie's teacher. I had no idea he's so fascinated by her.

Not that I can blame the kid. I've discovered she has many layers beneath that happy-go-lucky exterior. I figure I'd enjoy getting to know her too. Stripping away every layer.

I shut my eyes, disappointed by the way my

brain refuses to behave. I can't think about her like that.

"No, I don't think that would be okay," I say, folding my arms. "How about we go to Elle's Bakery and stuff our faces with chocolate fudge squares, instead?"

Brodie pulls a face. "Mom says the food there is bad for you."

I resist the urge to roll my eyes but fail to keep my mouth closed this time. "What is this, has Mom got you on a diet? You're five years old, for crying out loud."

A door bangs in the distance and Brodie jumps. "What was that?" he asks.

I imagine it was Chessy making a signal that the coast is clear. I give Brodie a reassuring smile. "I don't know, but I'll go check it out. Then we'll get you ready for that shower."

9

CHESSY

I press my back against the new door to my apartment and take deep breaths, willing my racing heart to slow down. That was too close.

I know I shouldn't have looked, and I definitely shouldn't have looked twice, but I was standing in the shower with the hottest naked man I've literally ever seen.

The male anatomy is so interesting. I've never seen it up close before.

I tell myself I'm a teacher, which means I'm a student of all things. I was merely observing Jack's beautiful intimate body parts for the sake of science.

He was smoldering.

I swear he was thinking about doing something reckless in the shower with me. I could tell. And I don't think I would have stopped him either if he'd tried. A part of me, a teeny-tiny part, is disappointed he didn't make a move.

My stomach lurches at what happened next.

I snuck out of Jack's apartment unnoticed. I honestly have no idea how I managed to do that. Every tiptoe threatened to make a floorboard creak, and when I got a slight tickle in the back of my throat, it was sheer agony to suppress a cough. But I couldn't risk making a sound.

My sisters are right. There's too much stress and drama around Jack.

It would be easier on all of us to just pretend none of this happened. I can settle back into my role as Brodie's fun kindergarten teacher, and Jack can stay the grumpy guy next door who happens to be a dad of one of my students. Except I think I'll forever have a crush on him.

Then my School Principal will come back, Brodie will go to his mom's, and everything can go back to normal.

Ready for work, I successfully avoid being seen as I head for the parking garage. I decide it's worth going into overdraft for a day to get gas. After the week I'm having, I think I deserve to avoid riding the subway.

In class, I take deep breaths, putting on my best smile as my kids take their seats and we prepare to begin another school day.

This is just a normal day at work, I tell myself as I tap my pencil on the notepad in front of me.

But then the classroom door opens, and the Vice Principal walks in. "Sorry to interrupt, Miss Scott. But your car is the gray Honda Civic, right?"

I nod. "Is there a problem?"

The VP straightens his spine and interlocks his stubby fingers with a sigh. "Yeah, you're gonna need to move it. You're blocking the janitor's truck."

I jump to my feet in surprise. I was so distracted by the chaos in my head, I don't even remember parking. "I'm so sorry, I'll just go and—"

The vice principal raises a palm. "I'll watch your class until you're back."

It takes me at least ten minutes to find another space. When I dash back into my classroom, the air has changed. All eyes are on me, and I could swear there's steam coming out of the VP's ears.

"Come to my office during recess. We need to have a word."

He exits the classroom, leaving me clueless. What on earth happened while I was gone? I notice the kids giggling and pointing at me.

I pat myself down, wondering if I'm having some kind of wardrobe malfunction. My clothes seem to be intact. I made sure not to put on the pair of pants that has Brodie's red handprint on my butt.

Whatever is going on, I'm pretty sure Brodie is the reason. I spot him at his seat, gleeful and talking at top speed with the other kids.

"Good morning, class. Please sit on the carpet for class meeting," I announce. The chatter dies down as everyone finds a space to sit cross-legged on the red carpet next to the bookcase.

I'm going through the announcements for the day when a little hand shoots up in the air from the back row. It's Harmony, the tallest girl in class with a wild mane of frizzy red hair.

"Yes?" I say.

Her freckled face beams at me, lighting up the

room. "Is it true Brodie's dad saw you with no clothes on?"

My heart stops and the room explodes into fits of giggles. "What! I… no!" I stammer, suddenly at a loss on what to do with my hands. I stuff them in my pockets.

"But you were in the shower together," another kid pipes up. I look around, stunned as voices hit me from every direction.

"Why was Brodie's dad in the shower with Miss Scott?"

"Are they getting married?"

"No, it's not like that!" I say, waving my hands at the disaster all around me.

Brodie shakes his head and stands up, prompting the class to look at him. "No… Sillies." He places his hands on his hips. "Miss Scott was attacked by a monster in the shower, my dad got an axe and killed it."

The room gasps in awe.

Somebody asks, "Is it true?"

I'm trying to work out when Brodie is referring to—last night, or this morning? Both times, I was in the shower. But the second time, I was in the shower with his father. And that time, he was naked. Seeing as Brodie mentioned the axe, I'm betting that he wasn't asleep last night after all.

My upper lip begins to sweat.

"I think that's enough chatter for today's meeting, go back to your seats and pull out your books for reading time."

I chew the end of my pencil while the minutes tick by and the kids go through their picture books. I keep swinging between calm and panic as I think about what I'm going to say to the VP. Clearly, Brodie must have told the class about the spider incident. I'm sure once I explain the situation, everything will be fine.

But how do I look the Vice Principal in the eye and tell him I was not in the shower with Jack? If the man knew Jack was naked too, aroused no less, and that we were inches from doing something about it, I'll be waving bye-bye to my career.

I swallow hard during recess, waiting outside the Vice Principal's office to be called in.

I know I've not done anything wrong, but I can't help but break into a nervous jitter. My right foot won't stop tapping. I try to pacify myself by observing the door.

The blue paint around the metal plaque on

the door is peeling. The name *Mr. Hargreaves* is etched onto it.

The door flies open suddenly, and I'm face to face with the stout man. He has a pair of glasses perched on the edge of his nose and he gives me a discerning stare like a grandfather confronting a particularly wayward grandkid.

"Come in, Miss Scott."

I follow him into the cramped office and try to resist the urge to cough as a musty smell accosts me and clings to the back of my throat.

"Take a seat."

Mr. Hargreaves is a man of few words. It's a shock to the system just to hear his voice. So often, it's the Principal shouting at the kids—delivering speeches or speaking to the teachers in the staff room. Vice Principal Hargreaves is the quiet, calm one.

He's not quite so calm now. There's a look of thunder behind his smile. "A boy in your class told me some alarming things this morning…"

"I can explain," I say before he fires me on the spot. "It's absolutely not what it sounds like."

"Oh?" The man leans back in his chair and hums deep and low. "He said his dad went into your bathroom while you were in the shower, is that not true?"

I scratch an invisible itch on my arm and chew my lip. "Well... Yes, that's true, but—"

"And Brodie heard you screaming... Were you screaming, Miss Scott?" he asks. His voice is steady, but I'm convinced he's fuming inside.

I lean forward to give him a sincere look. "Please. I realize how all of this sounds, but you have to trust me—it's not like that at all."

Mr. Hargreaves gives me two slow blinks and I take that as a signal to tell my side of the story.

I suck in a breath.

"I was taking a shower, yes. Brodie's dad is my neighbor, you see. There was this huge spider..." I trail off and watch Mr. Hargreaves closely, hoping he can fill in the rest. His brows do not so much as twitch in response. I get the impression he's still not convinced. Sighing, I fiddle with the hem of my shirt and recount the rest.

"Jack... Brodie's dad, thought I was being robbed. So he broke in to save me. When he realized the situation, he got rid of the spider and left." I pause for dramatic effect and muster my most serious expression. "Nothing happened. I promise."

Mr. Hargreaves does not say a word. He just stares me down. I refuse to break eye contact for fear of looking insincere. Finally, after what feels like a lifetime, he unfolds his arms and clears his throat.

"Well, that being said, let me remind you Miss Scott, that you are still working your probationary period. If I find out you are dating one of the student's parents, then I shall have to—"

"I know," I cut in. "I would never. Especially as he's the Principal's ex-husband."

Mr. Hardgrave's nostrils flare for a second. "Exactly. So, we are on the same page, then?"

I nod like an over excited puppy. At least I'm not getting fired. "Yes. Yes, absolutely."

Mr. Hargreaves sighs deeply. "Well then, in that case, I see no reason to alarm the Principal with this information," he says through a heavy sigh. I exhale sweet relief. The last thing I need right now is for Jack's ex-wife, who is also my boss, to hear about any of this.

Though I have no idea how to stop Brodie from telling her about the shower incident. The kid thinks his dad is a hero and he wants the world to know about it.

"We'll keep this between us for now. But, Miss

Scott, if I hear any more shower stories about you and any other parents, I will not wait for the Principal to return to let you go."

I swallow and nod in all seriousness. "I understand."

I'm trembling as I walk back to my classroom. I think about Leila. When I tell her about this, she is going to freak out. The shock might even put her into labor.

10

JACK

I spend the day running errands, stocking up the kitchen with food and all of Brodie's favorite snacks, putting on a load of laundry and scrubbing every square inch of my apartment clean. It's all in a vain effort to wipe Chessy from my brain, but she just won't leave.

I curse the day I drank too much and let her in my apartment. Life was simpler when I was rude to her and kept everyone at a distance. Now that Chessy has fallen into my life, my whole world has turned on its axis.

One good thing is, I have my son back. Even if it's only for a couple of weeks. If I behave myself, maybe Beverly will allow more visits.

But if she finds out I'm insanely attracted to Brodie's teacher, she'll be ruthless.

It's not that I don't think Beverly will be okay with me dating again. Our divorce is final, so it's inevitable for us both to start seeing other people. It's just the fact that Chessy is Brodie's kindergarten teacher. That crosses a line.

I know the logic is sound, but my body continues to defy all sense of reason.

I like Chessy.

There's something about her that makes me want to protect her and make sure she's okay.

But it doesn't matter what I want. Brodie means more to me, and I can't risk losing him. I make a silent vow to be on my best behavior from now on.

I pull up in the school parking lot and catch a glimpse of her. My heart thrums my ribcage.

I clamp my hand on my chest to dull the pain, and a maroon Bugatti parks up next to me as I climb out.

I forget all about my worries for a second, impressed by the expensive car. The owner gets out. He towers over me and looks like he could actually squish a man with brute strength. I whistle. "Very nice Bugatti," I tell him. "Is she new?"

"Thanks, just picked her up today," the man replies. He shakes his hair out of his face, and I instantly recognize him as the Hollywood actor who seems to be in every action movie there is right now.

"Hey, I know you. You're Blaze Hopkins," I blurt.

Blaze waves a hand aside and looks down, modest. "Guilty."

We cross the parking lot together and I can't stop side-glancing him. "You know, you're my kid's favorite actor. He loves all your superhero movies. Does your kid go here?"

Blaze shakes his head. "Nah. I'm here to pick up my sister-in-law. She's a teacher here."

When we head for the same classroom, I look at him properly with my brows raised. "You're here for Chessy?"

Blaze cocks an inquisitive brow at me, then his face breaks into a smirk. "Chessy?" he repeats. Then his eyes scan over my body and his smirk turns into a devilish grin. "You're the neighbor she's crushing on, aren't you?"

My stomach clenches at the fact that Chessy has talked about me. And the high schooler in me is blushing at the idea of that gorgeous woman having a crush on me.

"Blaze Hopkins!" Brodie's delighted shout breaks our conversation. I look down at my son, who is staring starry-eyed at Blaze. "What're you doing at my school? Are you shooting a movie here?"

There's a gasp and Chessy appears behind him. Her eyes are on me, and her hand is over her mouth.

"Hi," I say, waving to her and trying to act casual. Chessy's eyes leave me and dart to Blaze before they move to meet mine again.

"Hi," she says in a strangled voice. I can see the cogs turning in her brain. It's the first time we're looking at each other again. With clothes on this time.

Not that it matters. We've both seen each other naked, and I don't know about her, but nothing can wipe that from my memory. Judging by her pink stained cheeks, I think she's thinking the same thing.

Chessy coughs. "Blaze, I thought you were picking me up from my apartment. I brought my car in today."

Blaze shrugs. "I thought I'd pick you up here

instead, saves time on traffic."

"But my car…"

"Leave it here. I'll drop you off here again after dinner," Blaze says.

Then he kneels and proceeds to have a polite conversation with Brodie, while Chessy and I have a silent one with our eyes.

I'm not sure what she's thinking, but I'm pretty sure she's not happy by the chance encounter with me and her brother-in-law.

"Are you ready to go?" Blaze asks Chessy as he rises to a stand. Brodie jumps up and down, excited. "You know my teacher too?"

"Sure do, bud. She's family," Blaze says, patting him on the shoulder. "I'm here to take her to my house for dinner."

"Can I come?" Brodie asks before anyone can say anything. Chessy's eyes grow wide and her face pales. "No, sweetie. We can't just…"

"Sure you can!" Blaze roars. His eyes sparkle at me. "You're both welcome. After all, my wife is dying to meet you, Jack."

"She is?" I ask, looking at Chessy now. Her cheeks are flaming red.

I'm so sorry, she mouths.

Blaze chuckles. "Sisters, am I right? They tell

each other everything." He nudges me in the ribs. I stare at Chessy, horrified. "Everything?" I pray she's not told her sister about this morning.

Her whole face is red now.

Before I can reply to the invitation, Brodie is charging ahead, leading us through the hall and out of the school doors. Now outside, a cool wind whips through my hair and I'm slightly dazed as we follow Blaze to our parked cars.

I want to come up with an excuse to get out of what's sure to be an awkward dinner with Chessy's family. But Brodie is so happy, running around Blaze's legs, laughing and playing with the guy. I don't have the heart to dash his hopes.

Chessy is walking as if to her doom, and she keeps glancing at me. I have no idea what to say. I reason we can stay for fifteen minutes, let Brodie take it all in and have a tour of the house. Then I'll come up with a fake emergency and get us both out of there. That'll leave Chessy to enjoy the rest of the evening with her family.

It's a fool proof plan.

But just as we're piling into our cars, I hear Brodie say to Blaze. "My dad is a hero too. He saved Miss Scott in the shower from a scary monster last night. I heard the screams."

Blaze's face lights up like a Christmas tree. He shoots Chessy an amused smile and eyes me again, this time with more scrutiny.

I freeze. "How did you...?" I begin to ask, looking at my son in horror. "I thought you were asleep last night."

Blaze roars with laughter. "Parenting 101, bro... Kids are sneaky little blighters. They hear everything and they're expert fake-sleepers."

Chessy and I exchange looks. She mouths the word *sorry* again and we climb into the cars in stunned silence. Blaze and Brodie look like they're having the time of their lives, completely oblivious to the fact that I want the ground to swallow me whole.

"**I** told you to stay away, and what do you do? You sleep with him!" Leila rants, folding table napkins in her lap. She's using her bump as a shelf for the folded ones, which would usually amuse me, but nothing can distract me from the fact that my neighbor is having dinner at my sister's house tonight. That scenario wouldn't normally be an issue—I like my sisters to meet the guys I'm dating, but this situation is different. And I'm freaking out about it.

I'm supposed to be avoiding Jack.

Things just keep going from bad to worse, and I can't seem to stop it.

"Shh. Keep your voice *down*. Somebody might hear you," I say, looking out the open door.

Blaze set Brodie up in his movie room with a Disney flick, and then asked Jack to follow him into the yard for some man-to-man bonding.

Leila rolls her eyes at me and jerks her head at the window. "They're chopping wood for the fire. They can't hear us."

Blaze took Lucy's boyfriend, Wyatt, out to chop wood, too. It seems to be his way of interrogating and scaring the heck out of anyone who dares to date one of his sisters-in-law.

"How much have you told Blaze about Jack?" I ask Leila, turning back to her.

Her bump is huge now. It wobbles like Jell-O and I can't help but imagine the twins are having a wrestling match. Her dark hair is swept up into a neat bun atop her head with a few deliberate strands of hair covering her ears.

She drops a napkin, rests a hand on the bump to soothe the movement and shuts her eyes for a second.

"I didn't get the chance to tell him anything, obviously," she says. Then she opens her eyes to give me one of her big sister looks. "I just can't believe after everything we said, you still…"

"I didn't sleep with him!" I hiss at her, leaning across the bed. "It's just a big misunderstand, all right? I was doing my best to avoid him and then Blaze waltzes into my classroom! How was I supposed to know that Jack's kid is a massive fan?"

Leila's eyes narrow at me and she gives me one of her lie detector looks. I lift my brows and stare her down so she can see I'm telling the truth. After a silent staring contest, she sighs in defeat and picks up a napkin again.

"Okay. This is what we're gonna do." She rolls her shoulders back, putting on her I-mean-business face. "We'll let Jack and Blaze hang out, then we'll have dinner, keep the conversation light and Jack will take Brodie home."

I nod along, grateful for my sister's quick-thinking, because in stressful situations my brain is as useful as a wet match.

"Great."

Leila squints at me with suspicion. "No flirting. You got it?"

I toss a napkin at her head and we both laugh.

LEILA JOINS US AT THE GLASS TABLE IN THE extravagant dining room. I sit, smiling at Brodie as he looks at the high ceiling and glittering chandelier in awe.

Sometimes I forget my sister is rich. Even though she's definitely changed since she married Blaze. She used to be a lot clumsier and goofier when she was young and single. Now she's elegant. Poised. Classy.

But I know it's all an act. Every now and again, the mask slips. As if on cue; Leila bumps her glass against her plate, making an awkward sound. The corners of her mouth tug downward and her brows pinch as she avoids making eye contact with anyone. I smirk.

No one else seems to notice. Blaze is in the room a few seconds later with a huge tray of smoked beef ribs. He places it in the middle of the spread and she's beaming again like nothing happened.

Her eyes find him and they sparkle. He looks at her and his left cheek dimples as he gives her a wink.

They have so much chemistry, it floods the room.

Jack clears his throat and mumbles something to Brodie, but I resist the urge to look up from my plate, even though it's almost impossible. I'm sat right across from them and can see their figures in my peripheral vision.

"So, Jack. What do you do?" Leila asks as we start loading up our plates with food.

"I'm a…" Jack stops, prompting me to glance up at him. He rubs his chin, keeping his eyes on his plate. For a second, I worry he's choking on a chunk of meat. But then he swallows hard and picks up his glass.

"He's a heart surgeon," I say for him.

His gaze flickers to meet mine before he flashes a small smile at Leila and Blaze. Then he starts to cut into his food. Leila gives me a look of concern. I shake my head, nonplussed.

She doesn't need to say it, I can already see that she's dying to pry into Jack's strange reaction to the question. But it's obviously a raw subject.

Leila and I made a promise to keep the conversation light, but it looks like Blaze has missed the memo and is oblivious to Jack's discomfort.

"Heart surgeon. Man, that's a serious job," he says, merrily chewing his food. "You must work crazy hours, though."

Jack presses his lips together and his Adam's apple bobs. "Usually, yes. But, uh," he clears his throat and shifts in his chair. "I'm on a sabbatical."

"What's a sabbatical?" Brodie pipes up with his mouth full.

"It's like a vacation," I reply without thinking, teacher mode on auto.

Brodie gasps and looks up at Jack. "Are we going on vacation?"

Jack shuts his eyes for a moment, and I shrink in my chair. I don't know why I keep getting him into awkward situations.

Leila tries to rescue the situation with a simple question. "When are you going back to work?"

Jack frowns at his plate. "I'm not sure."

There's a shift in the air while Jack stares at his plate like he's not really seeing it. He seems to be reliving something instead. The veins in his neck begin to bulge and his jaw juts out.

Leila and I exchange worried looks. I know we should move the conversation on, but my curiosity is piqued and Jack's tortured past is on the table. I can't help myself.

"What happened?"

To all of our surprise, it's Brodie who replies. He says four words so candidly, it hits me like a lightning bolt to the chest. "He killed a man."

There's heavy silence and all eyes are on Jack now, who cannot look up from his plate. His temples are the same shade as Blaze's new Bugatti. "Is it true?" I ask, softening my voice.

Leila coughs, but I ignore it. I know the plan was to keep things light, but how can we just ignore the fact that Jack is hurting? Maybe he'll find healing from talking about it. And if Brodie knows, then what's the harm in sharing the story?

When Jack does not reply, I find his foot under the table and give it a soft nudge. Startled, his lifts his eyes to meet mine. But before I can ask him anything else, he pushes his chair back. It makes a sound like Chewbacca. Then Jack rises to his feet, his eyes glassy. "I'm so sorry, but I don't feel too good and I think it's best Brodie and I go home."

Leila and Blaze try to argue, but Jack picks up Brodie and leaves the dining room in four big strides. I sit, too stunned to move, while Brodie's protests grow faint. When a door slams, Leila and Blaze look at each other with an exhale.

"What the heck was that all about?" Blaze asks.

I rub my arm. "I don't know."

"A heads up about the job situation would have been nice," Leila says to me.

I raise my palms.

"I didn't know. I just figured he works night shifts."

Leila looks at Blaze again. "Should we go after him? He should at least take some food with him."

"I'll go," I say, jumping to my feet.

I hurry out into the hall and throw open the oak front doors. "Jack, wait!"

But I'm too late.

His silver Mercedes is already leaving a trail of dust down the drive.

"I'm glad you called, Jack. This has been a very productive chat."

I run my tongue across my bottom lip as I murmur in agreement with the phone pressed to my ear. "Thanks, Doc. Same time next week?"

"Yes. I think that will be good."

I end the call and sigh, looking across the darkened kitchen at the thin strip of light under the door to Brodie's room. The TV is on, and I can just hear another episode of his favorite show starting to play.

I scribble a note to remind myself of next week's appointment, then head for Brodie's room.

"It's past eight. Time to put out the light, kiddo."

I open the door and stick my head inside to see Brodie fast asleep in his bed.

Guilt rips through me as I approach him and switch off the TV. Another day has passed and I hardly spent any quality time with the boy. My two weeks are slipping away from me, like water between my fingers.

After we got home from Blaze's house, I made pancakes for Brodie and sent an urgent message to my new therapist.

My stomach was in knots and I couldn't control my breathing. I knew that rolling panic attacks were on the way if I didn't do something. Luckily, I got a call back within the hour and we were able to go over some things that helped me regain some control.

When Brodie said I killed a man, I thought I was going to vomit or pass out... Maybe both.

I don't know if those are the words Beverly used, or if he just simplified the situation in his five-year-old mind. But hearing them from my son's lips had such a negative impact on me, I needed to get out of that situation.

The truth is, in that moment, I was no longer in a dining room. I was in the operating room. The slab of meat on the table in front of me was my patient, with his chest cavity open and his heart pulsing in my hands.

There was so much blood.

And my hands would not stop trembling.

The therapist was calm and surprisingly non-judgmental after I recounted the situation. She told me it was common with PTSD. I had no idea that's what I had. Veterans had PTSD from fighting for their country, not surgeons. Or so I thought.

I just assumed I couldn't get my head out of the past because I was damned to relive it for the rest of my days. As penance for doing something unthinkable.

I climb into my bed and bury my face in the covers with a big sigh. When I inhale, Chessy's face floods my vision. My sheets smell like her.

I guess I should be grateful to Brodie for what he did. If I was worried about Chessy and I crossing a line, I don't need to be now. The way she looked at me was enough to shatter a thousand hearts.

I saw the devastation in her eyes, the shock. She looked at me like she was seeing a monster.

I'm pretty sure I'll never see her again.

Of course, we might bump into each other

in the hall, but she'll probably pretend not to see me. I'll see her across the classroom or the school parking lot. Maybe the occasional parent-teacher conference. And when Brodie moves up to first grade, she'll be able to avoid me altogether. And we'll be the awkward neighbors who barely say hi when they line up to use the trash shoot.

Just then, there's a knock on the front door.

My limbs are stiff and sore as I walk to it. Blaze had me chopping wood for ages. But all of my pain floats away when I yank open the door and see Chessy standing in the hall. She's holding a pile of Tupperware dishes stacked up to her chin. "Leila insisted that I bring you some food," she says, keeping her voice soft. Her eyes dart from left to right at the room behind me and I know she's looking out for Brodie.

"He's asleep," I say, stepping aside so she can walk in.

My heart is beating so hard, it sounds like war drums in my head. All I can think about is the fact that despite that bombshell at dinner, she's here.

She didn't run away.

Chessy carries the food into the kitchen and makes a beeline for the fridge, while I hover near the counter, wondering what's going through her mind.

She looks subdued as she busies herself with fitting the dishes into the fridge. When she's done, she straightens, but her eyes do not quite meet mine. They seem to hover around my chest.

"I'm sorry about…" I begin to say, feeling awkward.

Chessy offers me a polite smile while she rubs her fingers in circular motions on her arm. "No worries. We get it. Things got pretty intense."

"Yeah," I say, puffing out my cheeks. I gesture to the cabinet. "Do you want a drink?"

Chessy eyes the cabinet with a frown. "Probably shouldn't… Brodie is here."

"Right," I say, deflating even more. Even if Brodie wasn't here, it'd be wise to not fuel our simmering emotions with a strong drink. A calming beverage instead, then. "Will you stay for coffee?"

I don't want to be alone. Now that she's here, I need to explain myself. I can't let Chessy go thinking the worst about me.

Chessy's mouth curves into a smile and she tilts her head to study me for a moment. "I see where Brodie gets his determination."

She puts her bag on the counter and slides onto one of the stools. I take that as a yes and head for the coffee maker.

"You know, it's not like Brodie says…" I begin, filling the machine with coffee beans.

"Oh, I figured," Chessy cuts in, but her voice is too high to sound convincing.

I suspect she didn't know what to think and—judging by the way I flew out of the house without any explanation—I'll bet her imagination ran wild. I don't want her to go walking around thinking I'm a murderer.

Even though I feel like one.

The truth is, I know I'm not. I didn't purposefully kill a patient. But I do take full responsibility and I'll never forgive myself for as long as I live.

"You know, as Brodie's teacher, I think it's important that you understand the situation," I say, with my back to her. I can't quite face her inquisitive stare right now, even though I want her to know the story. She deserves to know.

She hums. "That's a good point. For Brodie's sake, it'll be useful to know so that we, as a school, can support him and his family."

I shut my eyes and grip the edge of the counter to stop me from falling as I begin to relive the day once more. "It was eight months ago. I had just finished a back-to-back shift—twenty-four hours," I explain. "I was headed home when I got a call."

"Right," Chessy, says, urging me to continue.

My mouth has gone dry. I clear my throat and run my tongue across my teeth. "I was called back in for an emergency. There was no one else to do it and the patient would have died if he had to wait until the on-call doctor came in."

The coffee maker sets to work, and I stare at the coffee beans grinding up. "But I was practically seeing double. My blood sugar was low… I shouldn't have…"

I break off and turn around with misty eyes. Chessy rushes to me and puts a hand on my arm. The touch softens the sting. "You didn't kill him. It wasn't your fault," she whispers, searching my eyes. Can she see the months of pain and hurt, the anger and disbelief?

"Just before I scrubbed in, my phone alerted me to movement outside my house," I continue, grinding my teeth at the memory. "I used to live in the suburbs, and Beverly insisted on having one of those alarm systems with cameras that connect to your phone. I thought it was racoons getting into the trash cans again. So, I took a look, but then I saw Beverly kissing a man right on our front porch."

Chessy's other hand flies to her mouth. "She cheated on you?"

I take a deep inhale. Retelling the story to Chessy is so much harder than doing it with a therapist. Her explosive reactions are fueling my emotions. There's now a throbbing headache in my temples.

"My hands wouldn't stop shaking. I was that angry when I finished scrubbing in. It should have been a simple procedure. Despite being sleep deprived, the surgery went fine. That is... Until I nicked a main artery with the scalpel. I panicked and just watched as the heart bled out in my hands."

I lift my hands in front of my face and they're shaking again. "I promised myself I'll never step foot in an operating room again."

Chessy takes my hands and squeezes them. "Listen to me," she says, finding my eyes again. She grabs my hands in a vice hold and looks at me hard. "It is *not* your fault."

I shake my head, clamping my eyes shut. "I know you say that, but you don't understand..."

"You're right," Chessy says, and I open my eyes, surprised by her words. She shrugs, still clutching my hands. "I don't understand. I can't even begin to imagine what you've been going through."

She releases me to run her fingers through my hair and tuck a tuft of it behind my right ear. Her touches send shivers dancing down my spine. "But I can see you've been putting yourself through purgatory ever since."

I swallow hard, lowering my gaze to her mouth. She's not wrong. I've been punishing myself constantly since that fateful day, and then Beverly and I got a divorce and she took full custody of our son. She said Brodie wasn't safe with me. She convinced the judge I was manic depressive and had a drinking problem. I could only have supervised visits.

And until recently, I believed her.

I thought she honestly felt that Brodie wasn't safe with me. But then I get a call out of the blue asking me to take him for two weeks. No warning. I realize now it was just her game.

"I lost my home. My family. My job. It's been…" I break off when I open my eyes and see that Chessy's face has zoomed in. She's hovering mere inches from my nose.

"It must have been agony," she whispers. "That explains why you were drinking the other night. Is there anything else that helps with the pain?"

I glance at her hand resting on my shoulder and she follows my line of sight. "Does this help?" She caresses my shoulder, then drags her hand down my bicep. All I can do is nod as a rush of tingles scatter through me.

"I know it's complicated," Chessy whispers in my ear, her breaths tickling my neck. "I know we're playing with fire. But I can't help but wonder one thing."

She pulls back to look me in the eye and I frown, wondering what that thing might be.

She slides her hands over my chest and rests them on the back of my neck. "The universe keeps bringing us together. I'm lonely… You're hurting. What if we're supposed to help each other through this?"

"What are you suggesting?" I ask, eyeing Brodie's door, paranoid that the sound of the coffee maker will wake him up.

Chessy hums in thought. "What if I can come up with ways to stop you from thinking…?"

Chessy's lips touch my neck, right below my ear, and I let out a shudder at the surprising touch. She pulls back to grin at me. "Does that feel good?"

It feels equal parts wrong and delightful.

"Yes…"

"What if I do this…" Chessy unfastens the top three buttons of my shirt, her soft fingernails grazing my skin, then leans down and presses her plump lips to my chest. "Does this make you stop thinking?"

I exhale long and slow, sinking back against the counter as Chessy teases me with her mouth, brushing her fingertips over my pectorals and opening up my shirt.

"Do you want me to stop?" Her hot breaths steam against my abdomen.

"No," I say in a pant. Chessy leaves a burning trail of light kisses all the way back up my torso until her lips find mine.

Then she presses her body against mine, smothering me with her heat. My lungs expel all of the air in me in one satisfied moan.

She is the perfect antidote to sorrow.

My brain empties of all dark thoughts and my stiff muscles relax under her daring touches. We shouldn't be doing this, but I've never been so relaxed.

How can something so wrong feel so incredibly right?

My hands find her hips and I squeeze, checking that she's real and not a figment of my imagination. She mews under my touch, and it's the cutest sound I've ever heard.

Just then, there's a loud thump from Brodie's room and the two of us tear apart like we were zapped by an electric eel.

I fasten the buttons on my shirt quickly and hurry to his door while Chessy stays frozen in the dark kitchen.

When I open up the door a crack, I can see Brodie's toy dinosaur has fallen off the bed. Brodie is still in his typical sleeping position.

When I return to Chessy, my heart races and sinks all at once.

Brodie is a reminder of why I can't give in to my desires. I have too much to lose.

"I can't do this," I admit, giving her a sincere look.

I lower my head, and the next thing I know, Chessy's forehead is pressed against mine.

"I know," she whispers.

We share a breath and stay quiet for several moments.

"You know, there's no rules against us being friends," she whispers finally.

My hands clutch her waist and I hold her like my life depends on it.

"Friends," I say, trying out the word on my tongue.

"I guess sometimes friends see each other naked, and it's not a big deal," I murmur.

We break apart and grin at each other. "Right," Chessy says, her cheeks flushing.

The coffee maker is done and I let her go to make us drinks. Then I hand her a cup and cradle mine, inhaling the comforting scent.

"When is your sister due?" I ask, trying to think about normal questions I'd ask a friend.

Chessy takes a sip of her drink. "Not for a couple of months, but she's having twins and the pregnancy is high risk. So the doctor put her on bed rest. They want to keep the babies in for as long as possible."

"Oh," I say. Lifting my own drink to my lips. "I hope everything will be okay."

Chessy's eyes glaze over and I sense she's thinking about something.

"Do you have just the one sister, then?" I ask, curious to know more about her.

Her cheeks bulge as she smiles fondly to herself. "I have another one. Lucy. She's in New Zealand with her fiancé on a Lord of the Rings tour."

Her body slumps suddenly at the end of her sentence, and a sadness takes hold of her aura.

I set my mug down.

"Come here," I say, opening my arms. Chessy puts down her drink and gives me a quizzical look.

"What are you doing?"

"I'm giving you a hug. Friends can hug, right?"

Chessy's eyes grow shiny and she sniffs. "I guess so."

I pull her in and cradle the back of her head with my hand while she clings to my arms.

A deep sigh escapes me. To my surprise, just hugging Chessy has the same soothing affect as her kisses. I close my eyes. "I'm willing to bet you're the baby sister."

Chessy pushes against my chest to give me a shocked look. "Is it really that obvious?"

I smirk and pull her back in for a cuddle.

I can see the real Chessy now.

I understand why she feels the need to act happy all the time, and why she cares so deeply what others think of her. It makes me feel guilty about treating her with disdain when she moved in.

She seems close to her sisters. With both of them moving on in life, Chessy must be worried about being left behind. Alone.

"You're going to find someone. Someday." I promise as we break apart one last time. Chessy's smile falters, but she recovers herself with a slight shake of the head. "Yeah. And so will you. Someone who will take away all of the hurt and make you feel whole again," she says, earnest.

We finish our coffees in a thoughtful silence, but my head is ringing with the echo of her words. All I can think is, I think I already have.

13

CHESSY

So. Jack and I are friends.

It's a surprising twist of fate. I've never been friends with a guy before. I'm not really sure I know how. In the past, it's always been love or hate. No in-betweens.

Now that I'm a mature adult, I guess I'm trying something new.

Confident, career-driven women have guy friends.

Do I still have a raging crush on Jack? Yes.

Do I still fantasize about him while I'm in the shower? Also yes.

But do I want to get fired, evicted, and never see him again? No.

So, I keep my crush in a box, hidden away in

the depths of my mind, and pretend it's not sheer agony to be in the same room with Jack, unable to tell him how I feel.

A few days pass and we soon settle into a routine.

We bump into each other in the hall on the way to school and make small talk about the daily news or weather. Then we catch up at the end of the day after Brodie is in bed. Sometimes when I go to take out the trash, I can hear the sound of my principal on speaker. She's loud, but Brodie is louder as he fills her in on the day's events.

So far, Brodie hasn't mentioned the shower incident to his mom. Much to my relief.

Meeting his favorite Hollywood actor trumps any other story. He takes great delight in recounting it with his mom over and over, until she can't take it anymore and hangs up.

On Friday night, I settle down for the night in my slacks with my hair in its usual messy bun. Then there's a knock on the door.

I trudge to it in my bunny slippers and peek through the spy hole to see Jack's Adam's apple.

I smile and pull the door open. "What's up?"

Jack's face relaxes and his eyes lower to my bunny slippers. "Cute," he says, pointing at them.

Usually, I'd be mortified at being seen in such a state. I'm not even wearing a bra.

But tonight is different. "Look, I'm just glad I made it to the weekend in one piece. Don't judge me."

Jack lifts his palms. "I didn't say anything!"

We have a stare down, then break into a laugh at the same time. I lean against the door frame and cross my arms. "What do you want?"

Jack thrusts his hands in his pockets. "Well, I know you're going to say no, so don't worry," he says. That's unlike him. He's looking sheepish now with his shoulders rounded.

"If you know I'm going to say no, why bother coming over here?" I ask, giving him a wry smile.

A door creaks in the distance just then, and I wave my hand at the old man down the hall. "Hi Bob!"

The man's wrinkled face breaks into a pleasant smile, but his eyes shoot daggers at Jack before he disappears behind the door again. Jack leans in close with a chuckle. "He doesn't like me very much."

"Why? What did you do to him?" I ask.

Jack cocks his head to the side with a hum. "I

think it's more a case of what he thinks I'm doing to you."

It's my turn to tilt my head. "What does he think you're doing to me?" I ask.

Jack meets my impish stare with a cheeky grin that reminds me of Brodie when he got caught coloring one of the table legs in class.

Jack smacks his hands together and the memory fades. "We're going on a fishing trip next weekend. Brodie would like to know if you'll come along."

I try and fail to resist a look of repulsion. The thought of sitting in a dirty boat, with a box of maggots at one side of me and lots of stinky fish on the other makes my stomach churn.

"I didn't think you'd be up for it," Jack says, reading me like a book.

"It's not that I don't love the idea," I lie, touching his arm. "It's just that... I don't love the idea."

Jack snorts. "Okay, well, don't say I didn't ask when you see Brodie tomorrow."

I nod, chuckling to myself, then I study him. There's something lighter about the way he stands. It's as if he no longer has the world on his shoulders. "How are things going with you two?"

Jack glances over his shoulder at his open door and turns back to me with a thoughtful look.

"They're good. Brodie is great. He's been telling my ex-wife how happy he is here and Beverly says she's going to let me have him a couple of weekends a month."

"That's great," I say, and I mean it. But just mentioning Jack's ex-wife tugs at my heart. She is a constant reminder of why there's a line between us.

There's a lingering silence as we avert our eyes and look around. I get the vibe that Jack isn't in a rush to go back to his apartment, and for some reason I'm not in a hurry to close the door. His gaze dips to my chest and his eyes darken with hunger.

We've been playing our roles as friends all week now, but it's been a secret friendship. I am Brodie's teacher while he's awake, and Jack's confidant when his son is in bed.

We have taken to staying up late each night, curled up on the coach watching TV. Jack talks to me about various National Parks and tells me stories about camping with his dad.

I ramble to him about the misadventures me and my sisters got up to growing up—from putting together lame home movies using our own sets and props, to skipping school for the mall. I leave out the depressing parts, of course. I'm sure he does too.

We've discovered two more sensitive topics to avoid talking too much about: my mom and his dad.

We don't talk about my mom because she abandoned me and my sisters when I was a teenager. And we don't talk about his dad because he passed away too soon, and Jack never really got over the loss.

Even though we keep our conversations light, I think I can feel our souls beginning to intertwine.

I like seeing Jack every day. If we can't ever be in a proper relationship and I have to spend the rest of my life hanging out with him as a friend, I'm at peace with that.

I'm sure as heck less lonely.

Jack seems happier. It's a win-win.

Until one of us meets someone else and everything changes.

I push that frightful thought out of my head just as Jack lifts a finger in the air and dashes into his apartment.

A few moments later, he returns with a bag and hands it over. "Last night, you said you were craving those chocolate fudge squares from Elle's Kitchen."

I hold the package in my hand like it's a trophy and I'm about to offer an acceptance speech. Happy tears prickle my eyes. "Are you serious, right now?"

Jack watches, beaming now, as I dive right in and grab one. The chocolatey goodness is bliss, and I let out a long, hard moan. "Oh *yes*. That's *it*, yes, yes!" I cry out with my eyes shut.

Then I remember myself and open my eyes. Jack is looking around the hall in alarm, checking that we're alone. I'm half-surprised Bob hasn't returned to shake his fist at Jack and beat him with his stick.

"Do you and those fudge squares want to get a room?" Jack asks, looking at me with an expression I can't read. Amusement? Disgust? Arousal? Maybe all three.

I grab another fudge square and shove it in his open mouth. "Try that and tell me it's not pure ecstasy."

Jack chews, looks thoughtful, then swallows and gives me a look of amusement. "It tastes good, I'll give you that. But I can't say it really does *it* for me. I'm glad you like them, though."

His eyes dip to my mouth, then he leans in. "You've got a piece of chocolate..." he whispers, brushing the corner of my mouth with his thumb.

His breath smells like chocolate and I'm flooded with pleasure once more.

I want to kiss him so bad.

His eyes search mine as though he's desperately looking for permission to devour me.

I take it back. This game of being just friends is stupid, not genius. We're only teasing ourselves.

And who are we kidding? The attraction between us is undeniable.

"You know," Jack whispers. "Sometimes, friends kiss."

No. They don't. Lucy's frank voice is quick to snap back in my head.

Despite that, I put my hands on Jack's hard chest. "I guess, sometimes they do... On the cheek," I reply, clutching his shirt collar. Jack's smile widens and he moves in.

I can't stop grinning as I think about how naughty this is.

His stubble grazes my skin as he gives me a soft peck on the cheek.

I can't decide if it's because I'm feeling a bit tipsy, or because I've lost my self-control, but the stirring inside of me grows big and wild. Suddenly, I no longer care about the consequences.

I reach for his face, struck by an idea. "You know when friends do scandalous things?" I ask keeping my voice down now.

"When?" Jack growls. His voice rumbles though my body. I shiver with delight at the sensation. It's almost as pleasant as eating the chocolate fudge squares. Almost.

"When they play truth or dare," I reply, winking at him. "It's Friday night... Is Brodie in bed?"

Jack nips his bottom lip and eyes me for a second, as though he's trying to work out if I'm being serious.

The thing is, we've been sneaking around all week and Brodie has never walked in on us.

It's made me over-confident. Sloppy, even.

But my brain is conjuring all kinds of dangerous ideas for dares. And I want to do all of them. Tonight.

Jack gestures to his door. "We'll have to do it at my place..."

That doesn't make any sense. Do what? Leila's concerned voice floods my mind. *Francesca Helen Scott, don't you dare go in that apartment.*

I know there's nothing but trouble waiting on the other side of Jack's door. But I've had a couple of drinks to unwind after a long week and I'm feeling a little daring.

So sue me.

Jack must have had a drink as well, because his inhibitions are definitely lower.

We go over to his apartment, and he's set up cheese and wine by the couch in the corner of the room.

"I feel a bit under dressed for this," I mutter, pointing at my bunny slippers.

Jack chuckles to himself, then he rolls back the curtain from the long windows and the two of us look out over the city.

"You've got such a great view," I say, marveling at the city lights. "My apartment overlooks a back alley and another dirty apartment block."

"That's too bad," Jack says, lifting up the cheese platter. "Now, for your first dare. I dare you to stuff your face with cheese."

I scoff. "Make it a hard one next time. I happen to love cheese."

Jack and I dive into the platter, stopping to take sips of wine.

"Okay, now it's your turn. Truth or dare?" I ask.

Jack reclines on the couch and rests an ankle on his knee. "How about truth?"

I twist my face in frustration. Truths are not as fun as dares. I have to really think about it, but then the perfect question hits me square in the face and I give him a smirk.

"Okay then, truth..." I lean toward him, cradling my glass of red wine. "Let's pretend there are no rules. No consequences. No lines..." Jack nods along, and I think he knows where I'm going with this. He drops his leg and sits up, waiting for me to finish. "What would you do... Right here. Right now?"

The question makes the air vibrate. Jack's gaze turns heated and wanting. He's like a tiger eyeing up its prey as he drags his tongue across his bottom lip and takes in my appearance.

"I would start by saying that you've invaded my mind," he growls, and it's the last thing I expect him to say. He almost sounds angry about it.

I rest a hand over my heart, shocked. "Me?" I try to look innocent, but I can't stop myself from breaking into a wicked grin when Jack nods. He edges closer, uttering every syllable slow and low.

"You. Consume. Me." He takes my hand. "I want to know what you're thinking. Are you safe? Are you happy? I've had a taste of you and now I'm an addict. I'll never get enough of you. I'll always want more."

"More what?" I ask, taking another sip of my drink to steady my nerves.

Jack caresses my cheek. "Anything you'll give me. A kind look, a gentle touch, a feathery kiss."

He leans in so close, his lips brush against mine. We breathe each other's air. "Do you dare me to kiss you?" I whisper.

It must be the drink again. This is why we haven't had a drop since my birthday. Because when we do, our defenses are gone.

I'm struggling to remember all of the reasons why kissing Jack might be a bad idea. I can't even hear my sisters' voices in my head anymore.

"I dare you... To let me kiss you," Jack whispers.

I don't move, but I also don't lurch away when Jack closes the gap and tastes my lips with his. The tip of his tongue rests under my top lip and he sucks on it for a moment before he moves to my bottom lip and nibbles on it in the most delicious way. My hands rest on his shoulders as he deepens the kiss, exploring my mouth until the room begins to spin.

I can't breathe. Gosh, he's good at this.

We're really terrible at being friends. Yes, friends kiss sometimes. But not like this.

There's nothing platonic about the way he's giving me mouth to mouth right now.

Yes. The love doctor is in the house and every bad break up I've been through; every heart ache, is healed by his delicious kisses. The delightful contrast between his velvet soft lips and his scratchy, stubbled chin sends a cascade of tingles through my entire body. This isn't just a kiss, it's a full body, things-will-never-be-the-same kiss.

Right now, I don't care about the consequences. Jack and I have behaved ourselves all week, resisting the attraction as it simmers below the surface. But the tension between us has reached boiling point and is now impossible to ignore.

Besides, I reason that anything goes during a game of truth or dare. If anyone asks, we were just honoring the rules of the game. You don't refuse to do a dare.

No, we're not in high school anymore. And yes, this is verging on crazy. But my heart wants what it wants. It's foolish to ignore it any longer.

In fact, I'm pretty sure it's unhealthy to bottle up so much passion. It can't be good for the body. We could get sick if we deny each other any longer.

So, for good health, we deserve this. We *need* this night together.

"I dare you to carry me to your bed," I whisper as we break apart to catch our breathes.

Jack's eyes flash and a look of concern crosses his face. But then he makes a sound like an injured wolf and picks me up in his arms. His hands squeeze my thighs and I wrap my legs around his waist. He carries me along the hall and we keep our lips locked on each other as we pass Brodie's door silently. Then we step through the doorway and Jack tears himself away from my mouth. He tosses me onto the bed and shuts the door behind him, sliding the lock in place.

My heart begins to hammer.

Now it feels real, and I'm suddenly not sure how I truly feel about it.

"I dare you to stay very still while I worship you," Jack murmurs into my ear. He's still playing our silly game. I arch my back with a delightful shudder as his hands trace circles down my arms. All of my senses are on fire.

I allow his woody scent to envelop me in warmth and focus on the pressure of his hips on mine. The short puffs of air blowing from his nose as he plants soft kisses down my body make me imagine I'm a damsel being ravished in the forest by an alpha. His strong hands roam over the curves of my body. I let out a shuddering sigh. All of my fantasies are coming true.

I want this. He wants this.

There's no one stopping us.

Under the guise of a dumb high school game, we've allowed ourselves to indulge.

I try and fail to stay still while Jack simultaneously kisses my neck and caresses my inner thigh. He is an expert at this. But somehow, there's nothing lustful about his touches. He's so tender and attentive to my reactions. I truly do feel that he's worshipping me and what's happening is sacred.

He seems to know all the places that will set off a chain reaction of pleasure in my body. Under my jaw. My collarbone. My right temple… Then my left hip. It's like he's working a secret combination to make something big happen. I'm his favorite game and he's got a cheat code to unlock the bonus level.

And I have to say it's working, because every brazen touch adds another layer of delicious joy. I'm almost floating.

This is all new to me.

Other guys I've made out with would knead my body like I was a loaf of bread and smack their lips over mine, sometimes smothering me with spit.

With Jack, the party girl in me is saying, *'Oh, so this is how a real man treats a woman?'*

I've never felt this way before with anyone. The room is spinning and my ears are ringing as Jack smothers my body in a million heated kisses.

Soon, my body relaxes under him, and my defenses are non-existent at this point. He could be Jack the Ripper incarnate for all I know, about to cut me up into little pieces. I wouldn't even fight. He has me spellbound.

I giggle as his fingertips slide under my shirt,

but Jack clamps a hand over my mouth to stifle the sound.

"You don't want to wake Brodie," he whispers in my ear, teasing his finger over the lace trim on my bra, tugging it down.

My scattered thoughts come together at the mention of Brodie's name, and suddenly I see his little face in my head.

Instantly, I go stiff as a board. Jack pauses and looks up at me. I stare back at him, wide eyed, like we are just about to do something stupid.

If I let things go any further, we might just make the biggest mistake of our lives.

"We can't do this," I whisper.

Every word cuts the back of my throat on the way out.

Jack stops and props himself up on his elbows to look at me, checking if I'm serious.

"You don't want to?" he asks, looking concerned.

I shut my eyes and wriggle my hips under his, enjoying the pressure of his body on me one last time. "No, I want to. Believe me. I really, really want to," I whisper back.

I open my eyes again, and sigh. "But if we do

this, things are going to get a lot more complicated."

Jack crawls away from me and a rush of cold air wafts over my body. I shiver, sit up, and cross my legs. "I'm sorry, Jack. I just… I can't. It's asking for too much heartache."

Jack nods, adjusting his pants with a deep frown. "I'm sorry, too."

I know he's in agony, and I feel cruel for leading him on so hard, only to make him stop. But he doesn't complain or get angry, and I'm grateful for it.

Part of the truth is, I'm not ready for third base. Let alone fourth.

Not like this; with his kid sleeping next door.

I'm still wearing my freaking bunny slippers for goodness' sake.

All this sneaking around is fun, but adding sex to the mix is just going to make everything ten million times worse. After all, to him, it'll just be one night of frenzied love making.

Maybe he thinks it'll get me out of his system if he just takes me right now. Then he'll go on pretending we're just casual neighbors. But for me, it will mean so much more. I won't be able to look at him without a strong reaction. And his rejection later on will break my heart into a million pieces.

I'm surprised the Vice Principal hasn't already figured out there's something going on between us. My crush for Jack has grown in magnitude all week. When he's waiting to pick up Brodie at the end of the day, he's the only parent I can see.

We sit on the bed in the dark for several moments until our quickened breaths return to normal.

Then Jack drags a hand through his hair with a heavy sigh, looking away from me. His voice is strangled when he speaks. "It's just that I love you so much, I don't know what to do about it."

I freeze. "You love me?"

It's the first time a man has ever said those words to me. I'm usually the first one to say it and then I'm very promptly dumped because the other guy doesn't feel the same way. Or he's not ready for the commitment that often follows such a bold statement.

But Jack just said it. He said he loves me.

Well. That changes everything.

14

JACK

My blood runs cold as I watch Chessy's beaming eyes glowing in my dark bedroom.

"You love me?" she asks, sounding hopeful and happy.

I silently reprimand myself for being such an idiot and letting my big mouth run away from my good sense.

"No…" I say, my voice an octave higher than it should be.

Chessy's shoulders rise and fall at a rapid rate. Her breathing is accelerated. Her heart is probably racing. "You said you love me."

"Did I?" I ask, sounding like Ross from *Friends* when he's in a tight spot. "Are you sure I didn't say I loathe you? I mean, if you think about it, love, loathe… They sound very similar."

Chessy rolls her eyes. "No, you said love." She gets on all fours and crawls over to give me a kiss, but I shrink back.

"I think we've had too much to drink again."

Panic seeps through my body now as Chessy comes onto me. She climbs into my lap and rolls her hips in a way that would bring any man to his knees. I let out an agonized moan and grip her thighs.

I'm powerless as she rocks in my lap, waking all of my needs and desires.

My head tries to lasso my wildly beating heart with the thought that the only reason she wants to take things further now is because I told her how I feel.

Nothing else has changed. All of the obstacles are still there. It's just hard to see them right now.

"Hey," Chessy says, pressing her finger under my chin and lifting my head to look at her. She bends down to plant a soft kiss on my mouth, then she whispers in my ear. "I think I might just feel the same way."

My chest explodes with joy as she wraps her arms around me. I drag my hands up her back and bury my head in her neck, wrapping her up in a tight hug.

It's true. I do love her. How can I not?

She's my sunshine on a rainy day. She's the sweetest birdsong after the longest night. The gentle breeze on a hot summer's day.

I think of the way she interacts with Brodie. She bends down to talk at his eye level and softens her voice. Other adults look down on kids and shout.

She's real and raw and the kindest person I've ever known.

Of course, I love Chessy.

That's not the problem here. The problem is that if Beverly finds out I'm in love with our son's kindergarten teacher, I don't know how she's going to react. Not well, that's for sure.

"I don't want to be the reason you lose your job," I whisper, pulling her arms away from my neck and looking at her again. Chessy frowns. "Then I'll quit. I can find another school to work for."

I shake my head, troubled. "We can't do that to Brodie. What if your replacement is a real jerk?"

Chessy climbs out of my lap and sighs heavily.

"You really think we can't make this work?" she asks, hope fading in her voice.

I shut my eyes, willing my blood to return to my brain so I can think straight.

"Let's just take the weekend to think about it, okay?" I say, rubbing the back of my neck. "I think I need to talk to Beverly."

Chessy stiffens at the sound of my ex-wife's name. "What are you going to say?"

I puff out a breath. "I don't know yet. But Brodie has to come first. No matter how much I want to be with you, I can't risk losing him. And Beverly holds the power here."

Chessy stays still and quiet. I can't see her expression in the dark, But I imagine she's frowning.

"Okay. We'll have some space. That's probably for the best."

Decided, I walk Chessy back to her apartment and we face each other, like two star crossed lovers on opposite sides of a battlefield.

"Can I have another hug?" Chessy asks.

I reach for her. "Always."

We share a deep breath and I kiss her hair. "We'll figure things out."

"Promise?" she asks.

We pull apart enough to look in each other's eyes and I give Chessy a reassuring smile. "Yeah," I tell her. "I mean, now we know how we both feel... It's just a simple matter of—"

"Working out how we can do something about it without destroying each other's lives," Chessy finishes.

We laugh for a split second, but then we share the same troubled frown. Our predicament weighs heavy on me, and my brain is already trying to think of what I can say to Beverly.

Chessy's hand on my cheek stills me. "Hey, it's like the old saying... Love conquers all."

I tilt my head and squeeze her waist. "I've never really understood how that one works."

Chessy chuckles as I let her go and she steps away. "Me neither, but I guess we're gonna find out."

15

CHESSY

Now I've got some money in my account again, I decide to spend my Saturday shopping.

New Jersey has the best outlets, so I get in my car and just drive.

But as I go from store to store, looking through all of the designer clothes on sale, my heart will not stop weighing me down.

By lunch time, I give up on retail therapy and pick up my phone instead. "Leila, are you busy?"

My sister snorts into the phone. "The only thing I'm doing right now, is growing a couple of humans while I watch daytime TV. You want to come over?"

Yes, I freaking do.

When I pull up outside Leila and Blaze's massive house, Blaze is outside, washing one of his many cars. He's shirtless, and the sun bounces off the bulging muscles all over his torso. The guy looks like an action figure.

Lucky Leila.

When I climb out of my car, he waves a jovial arm in the air. "I'm glad you're here, Chessy."

"Really, Blaze, it's not even warm today," I say, lifting my brows at his appearance. He's wearing a tiny pair of shorts that can hardly be called boxers, let alone actual clothes.

Blaze is unashamed as he rolls his shoulders back and jabs his thumb in the direction of the house. "Leila isn't talking to me, so I'm reminding her what she's missing out on."

I resist the urge to gag.

"Why isn't she talking to you?"

Blaze drapes a rag over his shoulder and sighs as he leans against the blue Jaguar. "I'm leaving in the morning for a week. I've got to do a quick press tour for an upcoming movie, and Leila wants me to stay."

I suck in a breath. "You're leaving Leila behind?"

"Well, she can't come with me. Besides…" Blaze says. I get the impression he's rehearsed this argument in front of the mirror… Probably at the gym while doing bicep curls. "She won't be alone. She's got two home nurses, a personal chef, three housekeepers, and a nanny on standby. She'll be fine."

"Where's the tour?" I ask, walking toward the house.

"Los Angeles, Vancouver, Houston, and back in New York… So I'll only be a plane ride away at worst," Blaze shouts after me.

"Well, I hope you two make up before you leave…" I say over my shoulder with my hand on the front door handle. I catch a glimpse of Blaze's smug smile and a wink just before I go in.

"We will. She can't resist this," I hear him say. My eyes roll of their own accord at that.

I walk across polished marble floors as I head for the master suite upstairs.

The faint mumble of a TV is my guide to the large, double oak doors to Leila's room. When I pull them open, I find Leila propped up in bed, surrounded by magazines and snacks. Her bump has grown again. Now it looks like she's got two pillows stuffed under her shirt.

"Come here, baby sister!" She reaches out for me, and I run into her arms.

In many ways, Leila is like my mom. She's always been the one looking out for my sister and me. For years, she put our needs above her own. Until one day, Blaze swept her off her feet and gave her this fairy tale life.

A tear leaks out of my eye while my face is buried in her neck. She smooths my hair.

"Hey, it's okay," she says, soothing me. I guess she senses all the tension in my body.

Will I get my fairy tale ending?

"What's going on?" she asks when I pull back. I pick up a packet of cookies.

Leila shuts off the TV while I stuff a cookie in my mouth and chew in thought.

"Last night, Jack told me he loves me," I say to the Egyptian cotton bedspread. When I lift my eyes, I expect to see Leila looking shocked or maybe even rolling her eyes.

To my surprise, she's impassive. The left corner of her mouth twitches and there's a twinkle in her eye.

"I know. He was here this morning and told us everything," she says.

I nearly choke on my cookie.

"Wh-What?"

Leila pats the empty space next to her and I climb under the covers to snuggle up to her.

"Jack and Brodie showed up this morning. He was returning my Tupperware and apologized for leaving so abruptly at dinner."

I yank the covers up to my chin as I stew on this revelation. "He didn't tell me he was planning to come back."

Leila grins. "Well, he didn't want me to tell you that he came either. But sisters don't keep secrets from each other, and he should know better than to ask."

I chuckle, but then my brain explodes with questions.

What did he say? Did he tell her about last night? Did he tell her what he's going to say to his ex-wife? Did he say everything in front of Brodie?

Leila starts to stroke my hair with a soft laugh, as though she can read my thoughts.

"Blaze took Brodie to his garage to see his car collection, while Jack stood right there," she points to the bedroom doors. "He told me he's hopelessly in love with you and has no idea how to deal with it."

I hold my breath as I listen, clinging to every

word coming out of my sister's mouth. When I don't say anything, Leila carries on.

"I was so shocked; I thought my waters broke. Turns out I just peed a little."

I snort. Pregnancy is the grossest miracle ever.

"What did you say to him?" I ask, wishing I could have been a fly on the wall during that conversation.

I look at the doors, picturing Jack standing there with his hands in his pockets, leaning against the frame.

Leila yawns and stretches like a cat, breaking the mental image. "He said that everything is complicated. He talked about the trial and how stressed he's been about—"

"The trial?" I blurt.

Then it hits me.

The surgery that went wrong... I guess the family must have sued.

"You know, it wasn't his fault," I say, looking at Leila with sincerity. "He'd just found out his wife was cheating on him and he hadn't slept for over twenty-four hours."

Leila nods. "He told me."

I shut my mouth. "Okay..."

I can tell there's more that Leila isn't saying, but she just chews her lip and looks down. She's going through some sort of battle on whether to divulge any more. "Sisters don't keep secrets from each other, remember?" I give her a nudge.

She grins at me.

"That's right. Now, what have I missed?"

Leila and I look up in surprise at Lucy standing in the doorway.

We cry out in happy surprise and reach for her as she runs to the bed. Then the three of us hold on to each other in a tight group hug.

"What are you doing here? I thought you weren't coming back for another week," Leila says, her face turning red as she begins to cry.

Leila never cries, but pregnant Leila doesn't stop. Those hormones have a lot to answer for.

I look at Lucy again. Her narrow face and arms are tanned. She doesn't make eye contact with us, but you can't miss the sparkle in her eye. She's happy.

"I missed you guys too much," she mumbles, looking at the spread of snacks on the bed. "So we came back early."

Her engagement ring gleams as it catches the

sunlight streaming in through the open blinds. I grab it and admire the pretty platinum band. There's a bed of three diamonds sitting in a line. They twinkle like stars.

"Are you two still waiting for the big day, or did Arwen and Aragorn finally get it on in the Shire?" I ask, grinning at my sister. Her cheeks grow red.

"We had separate rooms, like always," she says, glancing at me for a split second before looking away. "But Wyatt wants to move the wedding forward. We talked about it, and I do too."

Leila gasps like it's the most outrageous news she's ever heard. "But the Plaza Hotel is fully booked for two years…"

Lucy shrugs as she picks up a cookie and pops it in her mouth. "I don't want a big wedding. We're gonna do it in the town Wyatt grew up in— Snowdrop Valley."

Leila lifts the back of her hand to Lucy's forehead and eyes her with concern. "Are you feeling okay? Why the sudden rush? You're not pregnant too, are you?" Her eyes travel to Lucy's flat stomach and she studies it with suspicion. Lucy lurches away with a deep frown.

"No," she says, curt. "I just get stressed out every time I think about a big fancy wedding at the Plaza. All the people and noise. I prefer the idea of getting married in a little church and having a BBQ for the reception."

"A BBQ?" Leila repeats in a faint voice.

I chuckle to myself. For the past two months, it's been non-stop wedding planning. As the maid of honor, Leila's made it her mission to plan the whole event and make it bigger and better than her own nuptials. But I guess in all of the excitement, she forgot Wyatt and Lucy are both autistic. As the old saying goes, one man's meat is another man's poison.

In this case, bigger is not better.

"It sounds perfect," I say, clutching Lucy's hands. "So, when is the wedding?"

"Next weekend."

Leila and I gasp in unison. Leila's eyes grow red and misty. "You're having the wedding at Snowdrop Valley, next weekend?"

Lucy hasn't picked up on the fact that Leila is on the verge of tears again. "Yeah. We don't want to keep waiting. I'm ready to start our new life together." She shrugs, as though none of this is a big deal.

Leila places both hands on her bump and shuts her eyes for a moment. I know she's telling herself to calm down. "But I'm on bed rest, Lucy. I won't be able to come."

Lucy shrugs. "That's okay. I figured you wouldn't be able to."

I bite my tongue as my head swivels from Leila's hurt expression to Lucy's neutral one.

"Lucy, do you not understand how much that hurts me?" Leila asks, looking at our sister like she's committed the ultimate betrayal.

Lucy frowns. "No?"

Lucy can seem like a real jerk sometimes. But she doesn't ever mean to be. In her head, the situation makes perfect sense. The old church in Snowdrop Valley is much less daunting than the Plaza in downtown New York. She wants to get married as soon as possible and doesn't care if the only people who can be there are a couple of witnesses.

In her head, it's not about Leila, or anyone else, it's about exchanging vows with the love of her life and starting their new chapter.

I get it.

But on the flip side, I look at Leila's devastated expression and I'm flooded with sympathy for her standpoint. Luckily, Leila knows how to work with Lucy's blind spots, and she keeps her voice steady while she explains how she's feeling.

"I've gone into so much effort to plan a special wedding for you, on your request," she begins, looking Lucy in the eye. "I love you, and I want to be there when you marry Wyatt. Choosing to have the wedding while I'm stuck in bed is like a big slap on the face."

"But I haven't slapped you, and I didn't mean it like that..." Lucy argues, frowning more deeply now.

I suck in a nervous breath, sensing an argument brewing.

Leila shakes her head and softens her voice. "I know you haven't actually slapped me. It just feels like it. Because it sounds like you don't care if I come to your wedding or not, and you don't appreciate all I've done to plan your big day."

Lucy blinks for several moments while she considers it. "I'm sorry," she says finally. "I wasn't trying to mean. I just... Didn't think about that way."

We sit in silence, lost in our own heads while we brew on the conversation.

Then I'm struck by an idea to make everyone happy—because that's my job as the baby sister.

"Here's a thought," I announce, and both of my sisters look at me. "How about we have the wedding here? The gardens are beautiful this time of year, and Lucy and Wyatt can have another wedding reception in Snowdrop Valley later on."

Lucy and Leila exchange looks. Leila lifts her brows. "I'd be happy to have it here, if you're okay with that?" she says to Lucy, offering an olive branch.

Lucy peers out of the window with a pensive look on her face. "I have happy memories here. And if things get too overwhelming, I can hide in one of the bedrooms."

"Is that a yes?" I ask, hope building in my chest.

Lucy breaks into a smile and gives an awkward nod.

Once again, my work is done. Everyone is beaming again. Relief floods me as I think to myself that my own life may be one big dumpster fire, but at least I can still help my sisters make the most of theirs.

Leila pulls her in for a hug and squeals with

excitement. When they break apart, Lucy looks at me.

"What's happened with your hot neighbor? Are you in love with him yet?"

I bristle under the abrupt change of topic and her blunt questions. "Well, I think I am, actually."

Lucy rolls her eyes. "Of course you are. You're in love with a new guy every month," she says, mostly to herself.

Leila glances at me with a concerned look and pats Lucy's hand. "This is different. Blaze and I have met him a few times now, and I have to say, I think this time it's serious."

Lucy's mouth drops open. "How can you say that? Did your baby brain make you forget he's her boss's ex-husband? And a parent of one of the kids in her class?"

Leila shoots Lucy a glare. "I do not have baby brain."

"Yes, you do. You called Wyatt Watson four times on the phone yesterday."

I lift my palms. "Stop it, none of this fighting can be good for the babies."

Leila clutches her bump in horror, as though my words might actually harm her precious cargo. Lucy shuts her mouth.

I throw my head back on the pillow with a groan. "None of it matters anyway, because there's nothing I can do about it. Jack is going to talk to his ex-wife and I'm pretty sure she's going to fire me and convince him to dump me if he wants to see his kid again. So, I hope you don't mind me taking one of the spare rooms for a while, Leila."

Lucy hums in thought. "This ex-wife holds a lot of power over you two," she remarks, scratching her arm. "But what if the tables were turned?"

Leila looks up sharply. "Are you thinking…?"

Lucy nods to her. "Yep."

Leila's hands fly to her mouth and she gasps. I look from her to Lucy, wondering what the heck they're talking about. "What? How can the tables be turned?"

Leila and Lucy look at me with identical expressions of triumph. "Get married."

I crawl out from the covers and get to my feet just to get a good look at them. "Okay, who are you both? And what have you done with my sisters?"

I begin to pace the room, my body flooding with jitters. Eloping with a guy I hardly know sounds like a plan *I* would come up with, not my sensible sisters.

Now I have to be the reasonable one? This isn't right.

I pause, look up at them, and open my mouth to speak. Nothing comes out.

They just stare at me with identically calm expressions.

I begin to pace again, hyperventilating now.

"How the *heck* can we pull that off?" I ask the room in general. "I mean, what are we supposed to say when Beverly comes back? *'Surprise! We eloped! Now I'm Brodie's stepmom and there's nothing you can do about it!'*"

"Exactly," Lucy says, her eyes bright. "She can't fire you for being married to the dad of one of her students, and she can't stop Jack from seeing their kid just because he eloped with you. You had background checks and stuff when she hired you, so if she's happy to trust you with a classroom full of kids, then the judge won't believe it if she says Brodie isn't safe with you. Besides, isn't he in your class?"

I shake my head, dazed as I consider it.

In a crazy way, Lucy's logic makes a lot of sense.

"It's really not a bad idea," Leila says.

I swivel round to give her an incredulous look. "Oh sure. I'll just call Jack up now, shall I? *Hey, I know we've only been neighbors for a couple of months... But what do you think about getting hitched?*"

"You could go to Atlantic City!" Lucy says, mistaking my sarcasm for enthusiasm.

Leila frowns at her. "I'm not missing out on my baby sister's wedding, either."

"How about a double wedding?" Lucy proposes. Leila's brows lift so high, they disappear under her wispy bangs. "You'd be okay with that?"

Lucy shrugs. "I don't care. It's less attention on me and you don't miss out on the wedding. It's a win-win."

I cross my arms and let out a dark laugh. "You're both talking like Jack is onboard with this plan."

Leila cocks her head to the side with a sigh. "He looked like a desperate man this morning, I think if you pitched it to him right, he'd jump at the opportunity."

My heartbeat speeds up as I remember what Jack told me he planned to do. "I need to go," I blurt, realization dawning on me. "I need to speak to him before he tells Beverly the truth."

He needs to know there's another way out of this sticky situation. One that doesn't poke the sleeping dragon.

Leila and Lucy are smiling as I dash out of the door. "Go get your man, girl!" one of them calls out.

But I stop in my tracks at the sight of Blaze and Wyatt talking in the entrance hall and circle back.

"Oh, and Leila," I say, popping my head into her room. Leila looks up from the bed.

"Make up with your husband, will you? He's acting weird."

Leila's face floods with color as she laughs. "I'm not actually mad at him. I just like it when he grovels. It really spices things up in the bedroom."

"But you're so... Pregnant!" Lucy blurts, her face twisting.

Leila points at herself. "Look at me. I'm stuck in this stupid bed for weeks. I need to do something. And when Blaze thinks he's in trouble, he worships me like a goddess... sometimes he does this thing with his knuckles down my spine—"

Lucy and I make identical sounds of repulsion. "Just stop. Please, I can't take it," I say waving my hands. Lucy has hers over her ears with a grimace.

I hurry away, my mind set on the mission ahead. I need to speak to Jack before it's too late.

16

JACK

I'm sat in my kitchen with a mug of steaming coffee in my hands while Brodie speaks with his mom on the phone. Their voices are muted by the sound of my thoughts; one memory in particular, sparked by the freshly ground coffee flooding my senses.

It was dark outside. The soft LED lights under the cabinets were the only source of light in the quiet kitchen as Chessy and I stood with our coffee mugs, sizing each other up.

I can still taste her lip balm. The sweet memory of kissing her warms my chest.

It's been so long since anyone made me feel this kind of warmth. I almost forgot what it's like to be loved.

Then I remember I've not yet worked out how to broach the topic with Beverly. My stomach churns. It's been ten transformational days since Brodie came to stay. Just ten days. Yet, it seems like years.

I'm no longer relying on hard liquor to make it through the night or sleeping in past noon. I'm not alone and plagued with the nightmares of my past mistakes.

Beverly's betrayal has lost its sting. But I think the sound of her voice will always grate on me.

The best part is, I feel human again.

I open the blinds in the morning and reach for the coffee maker instead of a bottle.

I shop for groceries. I cook. I take care of myself.

Brodie has given me a sense of purpose, and Chessy's bubbly company has given me so much light. Her smile is like the sunrise—bright and hopeful. I could happily bathe in the heat of her gaze.

The meeting at the hospital is just three days away, and despite my doubts, I think I'm ready to go back. I'm not sure in what capacity yet. Probably not cutting right away. But the idea of going back to work does not flood me with dread like it once did. I'm in therapy after all, feeling better about my life. I find myself lying in bed daydreaming about performing double by-passes again.

That's got to be a good sign.

And my fingers occasionally twitch—telling me that no matter how much I want to pretend I don't want it... I'm a surgeon. It's who I am. I'm the *best* heart surgeon on the East Coast. The urge to go back to work gets stronger every day.

I'm on the precipice of having it all—regular contact with my son, the satisfaction of my work, and a beautiful, funny woman to share my life with.

Still, Beverly is standing in the way. She holds the cards.

If I make one wrong move, this tower is going to come crashing down.

The deep thinker in me wants to sit alone in a dark room and go over all of the possible scenarios. Hopefully, I'll come up with a more thought-out plan.

But this can't wait any longer. I need to tell her how I feel about Chessy. Falling for our son's kindergarten teacher in a whirlwind romance might sound scandalous, but it's nothing like that at all.

I don't see her as Brodie's teacher. To me, she'll always be the new girl next door.

After all, the night of our drunken fumble was after weeks of pent-up attraction. I was in a bad place, and she was there. I had no idea who she was.

If I'd known... If I'd even an inkling that she was Brodie's teacher, I would have never let her into my life. At least... Not until Brodie graduated to first grade.

But I can't go back and change things.

I can't pretend I don't have romantic feelings. We already tried that—and failed.

And I can't let Chessy slip through my fingers just because my ex-wife might take a grudge and stop me from seeing Brodie.

Maybe we can all be adults about this.

If I can talk it over with Beverly and stay calm as I fill her in on the situation, maybe Chessy and I have a chance.

We can go on real dates—no more hiding and sneaking around. No more lies or games. We can start a normal relationship like a normal couple.

Her presence in my life has grounded me. For

the first time in a long time, those dark clouds of despair above my head have faded. I have rays of hope in their place.

Hope for a healthier outlook on life. Hope that one day, I can go back to work and show Brodie what a real man does after he's beaten down. Hope that I can juggle work and family better next time.

All of that is worth fighting for. *She's* worth fighting for.

I'm just thinking that everything is going to work out, when I catch the tail end of Brodie's conversation.

"...Miss Scott was screaming when dad went to check on her in the shower," he says, innocently coloring in his favorite dinosaur book.

My blood turns cold as all of my hopes and dreams fall like rocks to the pit of my stomach.

"What? Put Dad on the phone right now," Beverly barks. She doesn't even try to act causal for Brodie's sake.

I watch my son's little brows pinch with hurt. "Am I in trouble?" he asks.

No, bud. I am.

My fingers curl into my palms as I cross the kitchen to Brodie. "You're not in trouble. How about you take my tablet in your room and play that game you love?"

"But Mom says I can't play games on the tablet for longer than—"

"It's fine, Brodie," Beverly's voice cuts in, her voice crackling in the speaker. "Your dad and I need to talk about boring, grown-up stuff."

Brodie's face turns gleeful as he yanks the tablet from the coffee table and dashes down the hall to his room. I let out a breath at the sound of the door slamming shut and brace myself for the conversation I'd been dreading. I'm flooded with irritation at the fact I need to explain myself at all. What I do in my private time is my business, not hers. I don't owe her an explanation.

I'm a single man now. I could have three women in the shower with me if I want.

I have to take a deep breath to calm down. Beverly is the mother of my child, and her little boy just told her that he heard screaming.

On that count, she deserves to know I've not been irresponsible around our son.

I put the phone to my ear. "Listen, nothing happened. It's just a big misunderstanding. In fact, it's funny if you think about it. Chessy was scared of a spider..."

"Chessy?" Beverly repeats, sounding utterly disgusted. I curse my own stupidity. How could I have let that slip?

"Miss Scott," I add. But it's too late and the damage is already done.

"Since when have you been calling her Chessy?" Beverly says, sounding like a cop.

I start to pace the room to get rid of all the pent-up nerves in my body. "How was I supposed to know she works at your school? She lives across the hall from me, remember?"

"How long have you two been seeing each other?" Beverly asks, her voice strained. I can pick up a hint of hurt in her tone now and my jaw clenches.

Then I'm struck by a thought. This is my get-out-of-jail-free card.

If I tell Beverly that Chessy and I have been dating long before Brodie came to stay with me, then I'm off the hook. It was an honest relationship, and she's the only person to blame for the situation because she kept me from seeing Brodie during the week. She didn't want me to be involved with his education, so there's no way I could have known that Chessy is his teacher.

That's on her.

"We hit things off as soon as she moved in a few months ago," I lie. "And to be honest, things are getting pretty serious between us." Which is true.

"Does Brodie know?"

"No. We've been very discreet," I say. As soon as the words leave my mouth, I regret them. I wish I could pluck them out of the air and take them back.

There's a hiss on the phone and I don't need to see Beverly to know she's sucking the air through her clenched teeth and squinting.

"How thoughtful of you," she says, her voice dripping with sarcasm.

I rub the back of my neck, picking up my pace. "I was going to talk to you about it."

Beverly snorts. "When? After the wedding? Or the birth of your first-born child? Or maybe at Brodie's graduation?" Beverly is fuming now. She spits words out like they're daggers, and every one of them jabs me in the chest.

"I'm sorry," is all I can say. I come to a halt before I wear a hole in the floor.

"You will be," Beverly says in an acid tone. Then she ends the call before I can ask her what she means by that.

My chest deflates as I let out a heavy sigh.

Despite my best efforts, Beverly is on the war path. Which means I've got a fight on my hands. The idea that she would be perfectly fine with me secretly seeing Brodie's teacher was a bit naive.

But there is one positive in all of this: the secret is out now.

No more sneaking around. No more restraining ourselves.

My muscles contract with anticipation as I think about it, and I'm overcome with the desire to hold her in my arms.

As if my thoughts were broadcast out into the universe, there's a knock on the door. When I open it, Chessy's beaming smile greets me.

"I know we said we'd give each other space for the weekend," she begins, raising her palms in defense. "But I've got this crazy, off-the-wall idea, and I really need to talk to you about it before you tell your ex-wife about us."

A foolish grin takes over my face. Without another thought, I cup her face in my hands and kiss her.

The warmth of her soft body fills my soul with pure joy. We're like two pieces of a puzzle and she fits perfectly in my arms.

"You are so beautiful," I murmur after I let her go.

She flushes with color while I take in the sight of her. Soft brown hair falls in waves past her narrow shoulders. She has a cute nose—slender and straight—between two round cheeks, red and plump as strawberries.

I want to caress every soft curve of her squeezable body and I could die happy drowning in her pretty eyes.

Chessy looks around, biting her bottom lip. "Isn't Brodie with you?"

I take her hand and consider telling her that Beverly already knows about us. The game is up and what is done is done, so there's no point hiding it from Brodie.

But I'm guessing we have one day before the Beverly bomb is triggered and we'll have to deal with the fallout. Which means, if I don't tell Chessy right now, we'll have one day to be together in blissful ignorance of what happens next.

I decide not to tell her. I'm going to savor every second of the time we have left instead.

"Brodie is in his room. We should go in and tell him about us," I say boldly.

Chessy's brow arches at me. "Are you feeling okay?" she asks, looking at me like I've sprouted two heads. "Why the sudden change of heart?"

I distract her concern with another kiss, drinking in the scent of her coconut shampoo as her hair curtains around my face. My right hand finds the back of her neck and I slide my left one around her waist, pulling her to me. Her hips bump mine and the pressure of her soft bosom against my hard chest transcends me up to heaven.

When we break apart, Chessy's face is flushed and she's out of breath. Satisfied that I've successfully avoided her question, I give her a cocky grin.

"Come on," I say, yanking on her hand. "It's time to tell him."

17

CHESSY

The door to Brodie's bedroom—which has always remained closed whenever I've come over—swings open for the first time, and I peer inside to see a young, dark-haired boy sitting cross-legged on a massive double bed that almost takes up the whole room.

There's a small lava lamp on a nightstand beside the bed, and a single chest of drawers on the opposite wall. A few toys lie littered on the carpeted floor.

"Miss Scott!" Brodie looks up from his tablet and grins wide at the sight of me. My heart swells. He swings his legs round and hops off the bed with a thump. Then he picks up a dinosaur from the floor. "This is my T-

Rex," he says, excited as he holds it up for me.

"Oh, that's nice. Does he have a name?" I ask, kneeling to his level.

Brodie frowns and looks at the toy for a long moment, considering the thought.

Jack and I glance at each other with a knowing smile, until Brodie makes a sound of triumph as if he's solved a riddle.

"No, because he is a dinosaur. Dinosaurs don't have names."

"How silly of me," I say with a chuckle. Brodie zooms across the room to pick up another dinosaur model. "This is a tar-an-don..." he says, getting tongue tied as he holds it up like a trophy.

"Pteranodon," I correct him. It's hard to stop slipping into teacher mode. "I like his cool wings."

Brodie stretches his arms out like the model and pretends to fly around the room. "Did you know their wingspan can be as big as eighteen feet? And not feet like mine; huge ones like my dad. Have you seen my dad's feet? They're the biggest, most ginormous feet in the *world*!"

Brodie continues to soar around the room, making sounds of glee while Jack and I look on with a smile.

"Show Miss Scott your feet, Dad. Walk eighteen steps and show her how big that is," Brodie says, pointing at his dad. I resist the urge to cackle with wicked amusement. Leila and I will laugh about this when I tell her.

"This room isn't big enough, bud," Jack says, looking around us. I'm impressed by his ability to keep a straight face. He pats his thigh. "How about we go and get some ice cream?"

Brodie's face lights up at the idea. "You can show us how big it is outside," he says.

Jack takes my hand again and Brodie doesn't even bat an eyelid. He just wriggles under the bed to grab a lost shoe, and launches into a barrage of questions, talking a million miles an hour.

"Can we go to the aquarium? Or the zoo? Can we buy fish for the sea lions? Can we go on one of those horse carts around Central Park?"

Jack gives me a quick kiss on the temple while Brodie rummages around with his legs sticking out from under his bed. "It sounds like a great plan for the rest of the day, kiddo," Jack says when his son remerges victorious, with a shoe in his hand.

Brodie's eyes move to me. "Can you come with us, Miss Scott? I know you're busy, but it would be real fun and we don't mind. Do we, Dad?"

Jack is beaming at me now, still holding my hand. "No. We don't mind."

I have no idea what's happening. Jack seems too carefree, but I'm still light-headed from the way he kissed me two minutes ago.

I can't help but be suspicious, though. Did he hit his head or something?

Did he forget about all of the drama surrounding us? Or is he maybe choosing to bury his head in the sand?

Out of nowhere, Brodie gasps and points at us. "Do you like Miss Scott, Dad? Mom says that boys only hold hands with a girl if they like them."

Slowly, Jack's warm hand slides out of mine, then he gets down on one knee and helps Brodie tie his shoes. "I like her very much," he says with fervor. "Would that be okay with you... If I hold her hand?"

Brodie looks thoughtful and I hold my breath. There have been many times I've wondered if I'm dreaming. This moment has to be the most surreal one of all.

My brain still hasn't figured out what could

have given Jack this sudden change of heart. I start to wonder if he spoke to his ex-wife already. Did she give her blessing?

If that's the case, then I'm definitely asleep. And if I'm in a lucid dream, I'm going to make the most of it and enjoy myself.

Brodie frowns. "Will Miss Scott sleep here now? Do I have to give up my bed?"

Jack chuckles. "No, bud. You don't have to give up your bed."

"And I've got my apartment across the hall," I add, lowering myself to my knees to join my two favorite men in the world.

"You'll be seeing Miss Scott here a lot more from now on. Would that be okay?" Jack asks. His voice is so kind and gentle, it stirs my soul.

Instead of answering the question right away, Brodie's eyes wander to the door and he grows thoughtful. Then he looks up at Jack. "Can I have three scoops of ice cream? Mom only lets me have one. She says it sticks to your butt and makes it big."

"Sure, you can have three," Jack says, and we share a chuckle, rising to our feet.

Brodie follows us out of his room to the hall.

"Dad, I think you eat a lot of ice cream. You have a very big butt."

I snort, grinning at the sight of Jack's neck turning red.

"Thanks, bud. Thanks a lot," he says.

The three of us walk hand in hand through the streets of New York. The whole world could be on fire. I'm in my little love bubble as Jack and I play happy families. To any onlookers, we're just two parents in love, walking with their kid. It's like I've stepped into the life I always dreamed of.

Everything looks rosy and sweet as we stroll around the Metropolitan Zoo. Jack holds me during the sea lion show, and Brodie watches the show in awe. After that, we each take one of Brodie's hands and pick him up with a swoop as we walk to the penguin exhibit.

My heart could burst with happiness. It's the most beautiful day of my entire life.

We share lame jokes while we grab ice cream and I help Brodie clean up after he drops some of his mint chocolate chip on his pants. Then we finish off the day by squeezing into a cart and look out at the lush green foliage while a horse takes us around Central Park.

Brodie's voice is music to my ears, and he

keeps piping up with little thoughts that make Jack and I laugh so much, my cheeks are hurting by the end of the day.

When we get back to Jack's place, his apartment is bathed in golden light from the setting sun, and Jack is still holding my hand. My heart is pounding.

"How about you put on a movie in your room, hey bud?" he says.

Being back in the apartment is like being hit in the face with a frying pan. All of my fears and worries come flooding back.

I hover near the open door, but when I do not follow them in, Jack tugs on my hand.

His thick brows lift expectantly. "You're not sick of me already, are you?" he asks.

I rest my head against the door frame and give him a small smile. "It's just…" I glance at Brodie, who is busy kicking off his shoes. Getting the hint that I don't want to talk about it around Brodie, Jack cranes his neck to smile at his son.

"You know how to turn on the TV, right, bud?" he says.

Brodie lets out a goofy laugh, like Jack has just told the most hilarious joke. "Yes, Dad."

After Brodie has scurried off down the hall, Jack turns back to me. "What's wrong?"

I bite my lip with unease and fold my arms, trying to vocalize the thing that's been bothering me since we got back. "Why do I get the feeling this day is a beautiful goodbye?"

Jack's mouth falls open, but he doesn't speak. His eyes glaze over, and I can see he's gone and lost himself in his head. "Jack…" I whisper. "What are you not telling me?"

Jack traces circles on my hand with his thumb for a few moments while the question hangs in the air. Finally, his eyes meet mine and he gives me the look. The kind of look I imagine he makes when he has to give bad news to a patient.

"Beverly knows about us."

18

JACK

Chessy blinks rapidly as she takes in the news. Slowly, she pulls her hand out of my grasp and a cold draft hits me like I've been dropped in a bath of ice water.

"Oh," is all she says.

I scratch an invisible itch on my jaw as I think about how to word my thoughts. "I'm sorry I didn't tell you, but I wanted us to have one perfect day together."

Chessy lifts glassy eyes to meet mine. "And it was. So perfect. I've loved spending time with Brodie too."

"He loves you. We both do," I say, my heart is sore from throbbing all day.

Every time I caught Chessy holding my son's

hand or showing him the animals at the zoo... My heart responded. It's been like a prisoner locked up for life, banging on the bars.

I tried not to think about Beverly today. I succeeded in pushing her out of my mind for a while. The result was a few glorious hours that I'll never forget.

But it was too perfect.

My mood lowers with the sun as I confess to Chessy that things might not be so rosy from now on. "We both knew it was only a matter of time before Brodie said something to her," I say, reaching for her hands. She pulls them away.

"I know," she says, looking at the floor. "But why tell Brodie about us now? He's going to be hurt and confused if things don't work out."

Her eyes search mine, but I'm not sure she'll find the answer. "You know, I'm usually a deep thinker," I say, putting my hands in my pockets. "But since we've been spending time together, I've been making a lot of decisions without thinking them through." I shrug. "For example, when Beverly didn't take the news well... I thought if I lied about how long we've been dating, that she would be better about it. But the way she ended the call makes me think we're not so lucky."

"You lied?" Chessy asks, lifting a speculative brow. I give her a sheepish grin.

"A half-lie. I said we've been together since you moved into your apartment. And it's half-true, because I've fantasized about being with you since the first time we met."

Chessy's eyes sparkle with sheer delight at my confession. "Wait!" Chessy frowns now, lifting her palms in the air and looking at me like I've just said the most scandalous piece of gossip she's ever heard in her life. "The day we first met, you told me off for making too much noise... I thought I annoyed you."

The corner of my mouth twitches despite my resistance. "You did."

I'm quick to clarify my reply at the sight of her horrified expression. "I was in a bad place, and you were this bundle of happy energy. It was maddening that anyone could be so happy all of the time. But I'm a red-blooded male with eyes and you're hot. So, yes. I fantasized about you."

Chessy lowers her hands and stares at me dreamily with her eyelids half-closed. "That's so... Romantic." Her eyes drop to my crotch.

I give her a firm look. "Focus."

She shakes her head like a spell is broken.

"Right. Your ex-wife wants my head on a spike… Got it."

My insides stiffen at the disturbing visual. "Don't say that ever again." I take her face in my hands and caress her rosy cheeks with my thumbs. My eyes dip to her mouth and the overwhelming urge to kiss her takes over me.

I wrestle with the idea while Chessy's hands cuff my wrists. She bats her beautiful black lashes at me. "My sister had this wild idea that might make all of this easier," she whispers, rising on the tips of her toes to brush her lips against mine.

We kiss, and it's the sweetest kiss we've shared so far. "Oh yeah?" I ask.

I'm all ears. If there's a grand plan to stop Beverly from taking Brodie away and destroying Chessy's career, I'm on board. I'm pretty sure I'm up for anything.

"We could get married," Chessy says, sounding hopeful. She blinks up at me with wide innocent eyes and looks unabashed. It's like she suggested we go watch a movie on the weekend. Not commit to spending the rest of our lives together as husband and wife.

I jerk away from her in surprise. "What?"

Turns out, I'll do almost anything. Except that.

"We can't just… My divorce is barely…" I puff out an exasperated sigh and scrub my face. "You're joking, right?"

Chessy's face flashes several emotions. I see shock, pain, embarrassment, and finally, fake amusement. "Yes, gotcha." She lets out a breathy laugh while I rest a hand over my heart.

"Don't do that. I thought I was going to pass out," I say, trying to catch my breath.

Chessy waves her hands while her shoulders jerk up and down with her laugh. "I really fooled you, huh? Yeah, I obviously know how dumb it is to even suggest the idea."

She gestures to me and herself. "Because we… This thing we've got going on. It's new and confusing and—"

"Complicated," I finish for her.

We fall into an awkward silence while I try to work out what the heck to do. I really wish we didn't talk about any of this. We could be watching a movie and making out on the couch like a pair of teenagers.

Chessy begins to chew her lip and play with her hair. "I better go…" she says, edging away from the threshold. My heart sinks, but I don't have it in me to argue. I'm going to need my strength to fight whatever war is brewing.

"Hey," I reach for her cheek again, she stiffens under my touch. "I'm going to fight for us. Okay? I'm not rolling over and taking whatever comes."

Chessy nods. "Great. Because I like you a lot."

My brain locks onto the word *like* and that sends a chain reaction of disappointment through every fiber of my being.

I've been downgraded. But can I blame her? After the way I reacted to her idea of matrimony, I'm surprised that she didn't call me Dr. Hart and shake my hand.

"Are you sure you have to go? I can make us some popcorn." I open my arms, inviting her in, and Chessy looks like she's tempted for a few seconds. But then she shuts her eyes with a frown. "No. I'm okay. I've got some schoolwork to get to. These classes don't plan themselves!"

I watch Chessy walk back to her apartment and hold my breath until she closes her door.

Then I shut mine and let out a heavy sigh.

Did I hope we could have finished our perfect day in the bedroom? Yes.

Then the bathroom. Then the kitchen

counter. And twice more up against the window overlooking the city? Abso-freaking-lutely.

But I guess nothing kills the mood faster than mentioning the ex-wife.

I hold my fingertips to my lips, savoring the memory of our kiss, and wishing that everything was simple. If only she was just the new girl next door.

We'd date for a few months, and then when things got serious, I'd introduce her to Brodie. I'd tell Beverly about her. Maybe we'd all go out for dinner.

Then, I'd maybe consider popping the question.

But Chessy knew Brodie and Beverly before she knew me. So, everything is up on its head.

Beverly is furious and heaven knows what that wretched woman is scheming.

A knock interrupts my train of thought, and a smile stretches across my face as I jog to the door. Chessy must have changed her mind, and I've never been so happy about it. "I'm so glad you're back," I say as I yank it open.

My smile drops when my eyes land on my ex-wife.

"You are?" she asks, clasping her hands

together. She pulls me in for a hug and plants a wet kiss on both of my cheeks. "Brodie, baby, Mom's here," she shouts, strutting into the apartment like she owns the place.

She dumps her leather purse on the counter and kicks off her stilettos while I stand in the doorway, too stunned to move. I can't feel my arms.

"What are you doing back so soon?"

Instead of answering me, Beverly takes in the sight of the apartment with a sigh of pity, then she struts down the hall. "Brodie, where are you, baby?"

There's a thump and pitter patter of not-so-little feet, then Brodie's door opens with a bang so hard it makes the pictures on the walls rattle.

"Mom!"

There's a frenzy of excitement as Brodie and Beverly embrace, then chatter to each other so fast, I can't keep up. Meanwhile, a storm of emotions is swirling inside of me, rising to the surface. Only, I don't know what form they're going to come out in.

Tears? Not likely. Angry shouting? Definitely not.

I end up pacing and puffing air from my nostrils like an irritated horse.

When they're done, Beverly follows Brodie back into his room. My ears are ringing with the steady *thump-thump* of my heartbeat. But the sound clears just enough for me to catch the tail end of Beverly's words. "…Let's pack your bags."

I skid on the smooth floor in my socks until I reach the doorway.

"What are you doing?"

Brodie is picking up all of his dinosaurs from the floor and Beverly is knelt by the chest of drawers. She's taking out Brodie's clothes and placing them in a neat pile in his open bag.

My heart hammers so fast, I'm not sure if it's from anxiety over losing my son or fury that Beverly is taking him sooner than planned.

I blink several times, waiting for an explanation. But she does not look up, even though I saw her shoulders stiffen at the sound of my voice.

It's Brodie who looks up at me with an answer. "I'm going home."

The words are uttered with such innocence that my first reaction is to offer my son a pleasant smile. But then the realization hits and my chest begins to ache.

I think about picking a fight, but Brodie is so happy to be going home, I don't have it in me to ruin it for him. Even so, I can't stop myself from giving Beverly a severe look.

"I need the bathroom," Brodie announces, tossing his dinosaurs on the bed. Then he zooms out of the room, leaving me and Beverly alone.

A few awkward seconds pass, then Beverly takes a deep breath. "Jack, Brodie needs a stable home. Right now, I'm the only one who can give that to him."

I begin to pace the room, struggling to comprehend her words. "What do you mean?"

Beverly rises to her feet, her eyes narrowing on me. "Do you know how hard it was for me to ask you to look after him? My dad needed me, and I needed you."

Tears well up in her eyes, and for the first time this year, I feel something stir inside of me when I look at her. Something other than intense rage, hurt or cold numbness, that is.

But I shake myself out of it to give her a frown. "I thought we came to an agreement. Yesterday, on the phone, you said I could have Brodie every other weekend."

"Well, a lot can change in twenty-four hours," Beverly snaps.

I drag a hand through my hair and listen out for Brodie, but when I can't hear his returning footsteps, I lunge forward and whisper at rapid speed.

"You can't stop me from seeing my son just because I'm in love with his teacher."

Beverly's cheeks stain pink and she lifts a horrified hand to one as if I slapped her.

"Did you say love?"

I swallow against the lump in my throat and back away. The tension in the air is palpable now.

"How can you start an affair with our son's teacher?" she whispers back with a hiss. "What kind of example are you setting for Brodie?"

I straighten my spine and fold my arms. "I'm showing him that it's okay to follow your heart and take risks. There's nothing wrong with that, Beverly."

"You're not thinking about him, you're only thinking about yourself," Beverly spits, her eyes shooting daggers at me. "You need to end it with her. Now."

I shake my head. "I'm not going to let you dictate who I can and cannot date. Chessy is kind, smart, and she makes me laugh. We're consenting adults, and I think there's no reason we can't be mature about this."

Beverly zips up Brodie's bag, grumbling to herself. When she's done, she straightens to give me another look, but this time I see a new emotion in her eyes.

Fear.

"End it. Or I will end it for you."

I shrug. "What's so bad about—"

Beverly takes another step closer, squaring up to me, her nostrils flaring. "What if things go south? You could be jeopardizing Brodie's education!"

I roll my eyes at the ridiculous thought. "He's in kindergarten. This isn't like he's about to graduate from Harvard Law."

Beverly drops her hands with a huff, then she drags a hand through her thick hair. "I was taking a risk letting you have Brodie while I went to my dad's place. I was desperate and had no one else to ask. But all I see is a man who is back on the drink, feeling up the new girl next door in the shower while his kid is in the other room," Beverly says. Her voice is calm and laced with disappointment now. "I knew you were a liability. But I had no idea you could stoop this low."

I open my mouth to argue, because she's painted the picture all wrong, but she isn't done. She lifts a palm to stop me.

"I know in your head I'm the villain, and I know you'll never forgive me for cheating on you. But our marriage ended years ago. It ended when you started treating me like a roommate."

I hold my breath as her words slice into my heart. The woman is so sharp with her words, I imagine my heart bleeding from a million cuts.

"I supported you during medical school. I didn't complain when I never saw you during your residency. I sat in the crowd and clapped along with everyone else at those dumb award ceremonies."

She pokes my shoulder with a bony finger. "Are you forgetting the fact you were in surgery when I was having Brodie? I barely even saw you when he was a baby."

I grind my teeth at her words. "We've been over this too many times to count," I snap, dragging a hand over my eyes to block out her judgmental stare.

The argument goes the same every time; she

tells me I'm never home, and not present even when I am. I remind her that she's always working late in her office and every time I tried to talk to her or show some affection, she would rebuff me. Over and over.

Her infidelity was just the final nail in the coffin of our marriage.

But this conversation is not going to help anyone. We'll just go around and around in circles and finish when Brodie gets back from the bathroom, and by then we'll both be even more frustrated with each other.

"If you're really just thinking of Brodie—and you're not swayed by your own personal vendetta against me seeing somebody else—then we need to talk about how we're going to co-parent like mature adults," I point out, stuffing my hands in my pockets and giving her a frank look.

Beverly's face is blotchy now, and her emotions play out across her face as she processes my words. From shock, to fury, to disgust.

"I do not have a vendetta…" she spits, wrestling with the handle of Brodie's bag. "It's a conflict of interest."

"How?" I press.

Beverly bristles and looks around like a wild

animal cornered with nowhere to run. The idea that I can't date my son's kindergarten teacher is ludicrous.

I know it. She knows it.

The only reason I wouldn't have initiated it, is because it's weird.

But there's no law against it. It's just weird dating someone who works for my ex-wife and teaches our son.

"This isn't over," she whispers just as Brodie's approaching footsteps fill the air.

"Mom, can Dad come with us to get pizza?" he asks.

Beverly's eyes are glazed over as she tugs on the bag and takes it out. I watch her struggle, too angry to offer any help. I'm not going to stop the mother of my son from taking him home. But I'm also not going to help her do it.

"Come on, kiddo," I say, taking Brodie's hand. "Let's get you to the car."

When we pass Chessy's apartment door, my heart jolts, but to my relief, it doesn't open. The last thing I need is a confrontation in front of Brodie.

When we walk out of the elevator into the parking garage, Beverly walks two paces ahead of me with her head held high. She struts with purpose and a confidence I now know is fake.

Underneath the hard exterior, she's insecure and busy concocting an evil plan.

But I don't care. If she takes me back to court and tries to paint me as a deadbeat dad who shouldn't see his kid, I'll hire the best lawyers in town and fight her every step of the way.

If she fires Chessy, I'll hire the best lawyers in town for her, and sue Beverly for unfair dismissal.

But then my body sags under the anticipation of all that stress.

"Bye, Dad," Brodie says, hugging me round the middle. To my relief, he seems blissfully unaware of any trouble. "See you later."

Beverly's expression stiffens. She doesn't say anything, but I know what she's thinking. *No, he won't.*

19

CHESSY

The morning sunshine peeks through my half-open blinds on Sunday morning before I even manage to fall asleep. Every muscle in my body is tight and stiff from tossing and turning. It was impossible to get into a comfortable position and even harder to stop my brain from spinning.

Jack's words made me break into a cold sweat. Beverly knows.

I'm kicking myself for running back to my apartment without finding out exactly what his ex-wife knows.

Does she know we've been seeing each other every day for the past week?

Does she know we've been in the shower and seen each other naked… Twice?

Does she know we made out on the kitchen counter?

I need more information, and I picked up my phone several times over the course of the night to send a message to Jack. But I deleted my message every time.

My body finally gives in to the exhaustion. I've just dozed off when my phone vibrates, and my body jerks awake again.

My head throbs, protesting against the rude interruption, but when I see Leila's name pop up on my screen, I pick up without hesitation.

"What's wrong?" I ask, glancing at the clock. "Are the babies…?"

"I'm fine," Leila says, sounding oddly chirpy for this time in the morning. "Why are you so suspicious?"

I lay back with a sigh. "Because you never call this early. Not unless there's an emergency."

And it's true, Leila is a night owl. She likes to joke that as far as she's concerned, time before nine a.m. does not exist.

Leila hums for a second, she knows I'm onto her everything-is-fine act. So, she gives up trying to make small talk and cuts right to the chase. "I was up all night Googling the law."

I yawn. "Sounds boring."

"I did it for you," she snaps, sounding like my sensible older sister and less like my hormonal pregnant sister for once. "Your boss can't fire you for being in a relationship with Jack. If she does, you can sue."

I snort.

Even though I appreciate all of the work and energy she's putting into my love life, there are some serious flaws in her plan. And the fact that she's blind to them shows me how quickly people adapt to life with money. Her penny-pinching days are long gone and probably wiped from her mind. I've seen her at dinner parties and BBQs with all of their rich friends. The way she acts, anyone would think she was raised in a palace.

"Sure. But I can't afford a lawyer, and the only training I have in law is watching four seasons of Suits. I hardly think I'll win the case by myself."

"I'll cover your legal fees," Leila offers. The idea makes my stomach twist into knots. I've never asked for money from anyone. Even when I'm down to my last dollar and have nothing in my apartment to eat.

I shake my head with a disapproving hum. Leila gets the message. "Anyways, that's not the only reason I called," she says, sounding sheepish now.

"What do you need?" I ask her. She doesn't even try to sound surprised by my tone. She knows that I know she wants something.

"Lucy talked to Wyatt, and the wedding is definitely on this weekend. Which means we have a lot of work to do," Leila says in one breath. "I will deal with everything at the house. The caterers, the musicians, the flowers, the cake... All of it. I just need you to do one thing for Lucy."

I hold my breath. "What?"

Leila exhales and speaks so fast, it comes out in gobbledygook.

I frown. "Huh?"

She tries again. Slower, this time. "Will you take Lucy to the mall?"

A bubble of excitement rises to my chest and all my worries scatter at the thought of taking my sister out shopping. The best part is that Lucy is rich now too. I can totally help rich people spend their money on themselves. I begin to make a list.

"Oh, I'd love that! I'll take her today! I wonder if the salon has any cancellations. We might get lucky. Then we could get her nails done. Do you think she'll brave a spray tan?"

Leila's light chuckle breaks my chain of thought. "I'm so relieved. I wasn't sure if you were feeling up for it with all the drama that's been going on..."

"Are you kidding? I was born to do this," I say, my chest swelling with pride. "It's a great distraction."

"Oh good. I'll send you a list of the things she needs."

My phone pings and a text comes through. Looks like Leila already had it written out and was just waiting for my permission to send it.

My eyes grow wide as I read through the items. "Lingerie for the wedding night?" I ask, my stomach knotting.

Leila sounds unabashed in her quick reply. "That's the most important one."

I end the call feeling less enthused about the idea of my job now. I love shopping, but helping my sister pick out lingerie for her wedding night isn't really what I had in mind.

Lucy and I spend the day at the mall. We walk until our feet ache, with our arms laden in shopping bags. I left the lingerie for last, in the hopes that I'd be in a better mood after doing everything else.

We get a free makeover at the big cosmetic store. Lucy gets a spray tan and mumbles about how noisy it is the entire time.

She insists on letting me pick out my bridesmaid dress. I opt for the cheapest one there. It's on sale—a simple peach number. Nothing too fancy, but it fits me like a glove. The cute guy behind the counter couldn't stop staring when I walked out to show Lucy how it looks.

I picture Jack at the wedding, unable to keep his eyes—and hands—off me. For once, I'm breaking my rule about not taking other people's money.

Lucy hates perfume, so we forgo that item. We get our nails done at the usual place we go to, and my heart sinks the whole time. It's always been the three of us getting our nails done. I can't help but stare at the empty chair beside me while Lucy tells me all about Hobbiton and some other random Lord of the Rings facts she picked up in New Zealand.

It's dark outside when we leave the salon, and my insides begin to wriggle. With a silent groan, I turn toward the lingerie store. "Just one more stop," I say, trying my best to sound chirpy and not horrified.

Lucy looks at the store and then at me. Her face pales. "We're not going in there, are we?" she asks, in a mortified whisper, as though I'm suggesting we take a stroll through Mordor.

Her reaction settles my nerves and I remember who I'm with. Leila is the one who always gives me too much information about her sex life. Lucy is the complete opposite.

She's not going to tell me all about the weird and wonderful things she gets up to with Wyatt behind closed doors. In fact, judging by the look on her face, she's just as embarrassed as I am.

It bolsters me to step up and do my part. "Let's get you something cute for the wedding night," I announce.

Lucy's left brow flies upward. "I don't think there's anything in there that I can pull off. Look at the mannequins… I don't look like them."

"You look gorgeous!" I burst out, linking our arms and dragging her into the store with me.

"I didn't say I don't look gorgeous," Lucy

quips back. "I said I don't look like them." She points at the skinny mannequins at the window.

"Exactly," I say, giving her a playful nudge. "You've got curves in all the right places."

"I don't think my gut is the right place to have a curve," Lucy replies, blunt. She pats the little pooch in her lower stomach. I roll my eyes. But then her brows draw together and her face floods with concern.

"What if Wyatt is grossed out by the cellulite?"

"Everyone has cellulite," I counter, but my words do nothing to calm her. Lucy points at me.

"You don't. You've still got baby smooth skin all over you."

I take a breath. Now I'm not sure what's worse. Leila talking about things Blaze does in the bedroom, or Lucy obsessively worrying over what Wyatt will think of her naked body.

I swear I'm not qualified for this job.

I pick out a cute, lacy bra set. "What about this? Shall we go traditional white? Or sophisticated black?"

Lucy touches the material and recoils like it burned her. "It's scratchy."

I put the bra set back on the rack and pick up

a soft cotton push up bra instead. "How about this? We could go for the wow factor and choose maroon."

Lucy hums. "Great. It'll bring out the red in my stretch marks," she says, sarcastic. She doesn't usually get sarcasm; Wyatt's sense of humor must be rubbing off on her.

I sigh.

This is going to take a while.

We walk around the cramped lingerie store looking at all of the options, and Lucy proceeds to tell me all of the reasons why nothing I pick up will work.

Too much material. Too little material. Too itchy. Too hot. Too tight. Too slutty. Too Bridget Jones.

My arms are throbbing. I'm still carrying the heavy shopping bags, and my feet protest with every step. I'm just on the verge of admitting defeat when Lucy makes a noise that sounds like a chipmunk being tortured by a bob cat. Then she dashes to the nightwear section.

"This is perfect."

I shuffle over, peering around the racks to see Lucy holding up an oversized shirt with a picture of the one ring and above it, the words '*My precious.*'

I smirk to myself. What are the chances there would be Lord of the Rings themed clothes in this store?

"I'm getting it," Lucy announces.

I almost argue that an oversized cotton shirt with a geeky Lord of the Rings reference printed on the front isn't the sexiest piece of clothing to wear on your wedding night. But then I remember who the groom is.

Wyatt Croft. The biggest Lord of the Rings nerd there is. He carries around copies of the books everywhere he goes, can speak some Elvish, and even calls Lucy "Arwen" when he thinks no one else is around to hear him.

"You're right," I say in defeat. "It's perfect."

Lucy pays for the last item on our list and we walk out of the store arm in arm, laughing.

Suddenly, my heart sinks, and I can't help but give my sister a worried look.

She picks up on the change in my mood and frowns back. "Are you feeling sick?" she asks. "You look pale."

I shake my head. "I'm just thinking…"

"Sounds dangerous," Lucy says with a chuckle.

We sit on the bench outside the mall while Lucy books an Uber. Then she turns to me with a determined look. "What's going on in your head? You know I can't read minds, right?"

I roll my lips inward and bite down. "Everything is changing."

She blinks at me, waiting for more. I rub my arm with a sigh as I watch the stream of people walking past. "Leila is going to be a mom soon. You're getting married…"

I look up, blinking quickly as my eyes begin to prickle. "And I'm… all alone."

Lucy hums. "Yeah. Change is hard."

I look at her. She's staring at the sidewalk with a deep-set frown. "Wyatt and I… Things are good. I love him. He loves me. I really like kissing him. But I'm scared about… The other stuff."

I cock my head and study my sister. "You two really haven't…?"

Part of me thought she was only saying they hadn't 'done the deed' to humor us. Or to put up a façade.

"But you've been living together!"

Lucy looks up to give me a determined smile.

"We have our own rooms." Then she looks away again. "But after we get married, I guess we should share."

"I think that's pretty standard... Sharing a bed with your husband," I say, chuckling now.

Lucy bites her lip and I push away my own fears to comfort her. "Hey," I say, tucking hair behind her ear. "You love each other. I'm sure you'll figure things out. Just be honest with Wyatt about what makes you comfortable."

Lucy nods in thought. "It's just..." Her eyes well up and she sniffs. "I'm going to have to share a room with a boy!" The last word comes out in a tiny wail.

I resist the urge to laugh because she seems to be serious. "No. Not a boy. He's Aragorn, King of Gondor, remember?" I say, speaking her language now. Lucy's face brightens as she looks back at me, delighted by my analogy. I give her a reassuring smile. "And he will treat you like his elven queen. I promise. He won't even notice the cellulite."

Lucy wraps her arms around me and we hug for several long minutes, breathing in the same rhythm. "I love you, big sis," I mumble into her hair.

"Love you too, Chessy boo," she whispers back.

When we break apart, it's her turn to give me a concerned look. "I'm sorry you feel like you're getting left behind," she says. Her words hit me like a dart to the chest.

I've never looked at it that way, but she's right. I'm scared that my sisters are moving on without me. Soon, they won't have time to hang out with me anymore.

I'll be all alone.

"What's going on with Jack? Leila says the ex-wife is on the war path," Lucy asks.

I take a deep breath and fill Lucy in on all of the drama. She listens and waits patiently for me to get to the end of the story. She doesn't speak until the Uber shows up.

She blinks slow and thoughtful, then places a hand on my shoulder. "You're always telling me that love conquers all," she says. "So, if what you two have is true love, I'm sure you'll figure out how to make each other happy."

We share a long look as I wonder what she means.

And while we ride in the Uber, I sit in silence, staring out the window in thought.

I do love Jack.

But what will make him happy? What will make me happy?

And when I find out what that is, am I strong enough to pay the price for that happiness?

I think about my sisters and everything they went through to get their happy ending. If I want to have a life with Jack, I'm going to need to be brave and stop worrying about consequences.

I pull Lucy in for a final hug. "Thanks, Lucy. You're right, love does conquer all."

20

JACK

I pace the empty apartment in the dark, too distracted to turn on a light. Ever since Beverly left with Brodie, my apartment walls have been closing in. The silence is deafening.

When I hear footsteps in the hall, I yank open the door just in time to see a terrified Chessy standing outside her door with her hand hovering in the air and her key inches away from the lock.

"You nearly scared the life out of me," she says, breathless.

I freeze under her stare, my brain unable to process a sensible thought.

I can't decide what to say or do.

My body wants to touch her and pull her in

for a hug. My mind wants to explore our options and solve the puzzle of how to have it all. Then there's my heart breaking at the thought of having to go to court again and all the drama that is bound to unfold if I keep seeing Chessy.

Instead of telling her any of these things, I utter two words that cut me on the way out of my mouth.

"Brodie's gone."

Chessy blinks. Then she unlocks her door and kicks it open. I don't need to say another word, the devastation I'm feeling right now must be visible on my face.

"Come on." She points, and I move on autopilot into her apartment.

It smells like her—Coconut and berries.

The door slams behind me and I don't get a second to process what is happening before Chessy's arms are around me and she captures me in a kiss.

It's the kiss of life.

All systems in my body start to boot up and my head is spinning.

Then she jumps up, wrapping her legs around my waist. On reflex, I grab her thighs to keep her in place. Our mouths are locked as we taste each other, soaking up pleasurable sensations.

Her hands roam through my hair, and her mouth leaves mine to sear a burning trail of kisses down my neck. When she tears away, her eyes shine at me like two spotlights.

"Does this make you happy?" she asks.

It's an odd question.

Any man would nod. I have a beautiful woman in my arms, and she is smothering me in hot kisses.

Why would that not make me happy?

Chessy grins before she goes in for another round of violent kisses.

She writhes, moving with such haste and passion that I start to sweat. But there's something about her frenzy that gives me pause. Alarm bells go off in my head.

Something tells me she could be intoxicated, or at least not really thinking this through.

Do I want to ravish Chessy? Yes.

But do I want to take advantage of her in a vulnerable moment? No.

Something is wrong.

I carry her to the couch and let her go to take a few deep breaths.

"Wait," I say, pressing my fingers to my tingling lips. Chessy looks up at me from the couch, her eyes stretched wide in surprise and disappointment.

"What are we doing?" I ask. "Don't you think we should talk first?"

Chessy crosses her arms. "I'm sick of talking about it," she mutters. "What good is talking when there's nothing we can do to change things? I'm going to get fired tomorrow. Beverly has taken Brodie away... We might as well enjoy each other tonight."

I shake my head. "You won't get fired tomorrow," I say, reaching for her hands.

She shrugs away.

I sit on the couch beside her and place a hand on her knee instead. "If you do, I'll take her to court and sue."

Chessy's eyes flash with annoyance at me and it takes me aback, because I have no idea what prompted it. But I continue my train of thought. "As for Brodie... I'll fight for him too. I'll always be his dad. Beverly can't stop me from seeing my own son just because she doesn't like that I've fallen in love with his teacher."

Chessy's eyes flash again, but with a different emotion. Her eyes are sparkling now.

"I'm sorry, I think I misheard... Did you say loathe or love? They sound very similar, you know?"

She places a hand behind her ear with a soft chuckle.

I take her hand, and this time she lets me.

"Yes. I love you," I say, dipping my forehead to press it against Chessy's. We both share a breath.

"I love you more," Chessy says, igniting a fire in my chest. Her other hand fumbles with my belt buckle, and her breaths quicken.

I caress her cheek and shift over to give her better access. The metal of my belt clinks as she unbuckles it, and my jeans button pops undone.

An agonized moan slips out of my mouth at the release of tension.

She lifts the hem of my shirt, and her cool fingertips make my skin zing. My abs tighten and my whole body goes rigid at her touch.

But I grit my teeth to cling to some self-control until I have clarity on what she really wants.

I want to be sure this is not just some spur-of-the-moment idea.

"Are you sure you want to do this?" I ask, reading the heated look in her eyes. "I don't want you to wake up tomorrow and tell me we made a mistake."

Chessy's eyes dip to my mouth again. "I've never wanted anything more in all my life, Jack," she says, climbing into my lap. Her weight crushes my hips, but the pressure is a new and delicious kind of torture.

My self-control is hanging by a thread; if she changes her mind, I'm not sure I can stop myself.

My hands roam her body, squeezing and pinching until Chessy yelps like a puppy. She throws her head back and lets out a breath. It's as though, all this time, she'd been trapped under water and her face just broke the surface. She takes in greedy gulps of air as she rolls her hips against me. I grip her thighs.

Oh, what sweet agony is this?

We both know what we're getting into. We've discussed the matter to death. And with Brodie gone, there's no one here to stop us. We don't even need to be quiet.

There's just one nagging part of my brain that tells me it'll be a million times harder to stop seeing Chessy if we sleep together. The moment we do, there's no going back. Not without absolute heartbreak.

And this time, I don't think I will ever recover.

Chessy leans down to plant soft, buttery kisses all over my face, eliminating my thoughts. I move on instinct. My hands slide under her shirt and I trace circles over her sides, caressing her soft skin. I move all the way up to her bra, slowly.

When my thumb grazes the lace material, she giggles.

Then I let out a breath on her neck and shut my eyes, clutching her back. For the first time in my life, I am complete. When I have Chessy in my arms, I feel like I can take on the world.

I hold her close to me, overwhelmed with the sense of coming home.

We kiss again, and each time our lips touch, it's like we're both offering a silent promise to each other.

I vow to protect her from anything bad. To lift her spirits when her mood is low.

I'll be there for her, no matter what. And I'll destroy anyone who dares try to hurt her or come between us.

She's mine. Now and forever.

I will die for her.

The last of my self-control snaps and with a roar, I pick her up from the couch.

I carry her to the bedroom, kick the door shut behind me and spend the rest of the night making love to her. I worship every single inch of her body until she mews and whimpers, unable to stand one more touch. We fall apart in each other's arms afterward, panting and lost in the exploration of each other's body and soul.

She is exquisite. And now that I know what it feels like to be this connected to her, I cannot imagine a day without her in my life. I nip her ear as she stills and begins to fall asleep.

"I love you," I whisper.

She sighs, content, and wriggles her butt into my crotch. I wrap her up in my arms so tight, I can barely breathe.

"Love you more," she whispers back.

I stroke her hair, watching the steady rise and fall of her body as she finally succumbs to sleep. Then I sweep a sweaty strand of hair away from her neck and press my lips to her bare shoulder.

"Not possible," I reply.

21

CHESSY

When I wake up, my brain struggles to compute why I'm pinned to the bed, but then I notice the heavy muscular arm draped over me and a flood of memories come rushing back.

It finally happened.

Jack and I slept together.

It should feel like another scandal—I know Leila will think so. But nothing has ever felt more right in all my life.

I shift my weight and throb, aching in places I didn't know could ache.

Jack's hard body keeps me enveloped and I shut my eyes, savoring this moment of just being surrounded by his masculine scent. This is what life is meant to be like—waking up in the arms of the one you love.

Hot breaths tickle my bare back and I crane my neck to sneak a peek at Jack's sleeping face.

His hair is messy and falling over his eyes. His plump lips are parted as he sleeps on, blissfully unaware of the fact that I'm staring at him.

He is so handsome when he's asleep.

I shuffle around and he stirs, but then smacks his lips together a couple of times and continues to dream.

I could lay still and stare at the man all day.

Just then, my phone alarm lets off a shrill ring. I jump so hard, Jack's eyes fly open in alarm.

"Hey," I say in a breathy voice. Then I grab the sheet and wrap it around me so I can hop out of bed in a home-made sarong. Jack watches with a smirk as I shuffle around my room, looking for the clothes we shed in haste the night before.

My temples throb when I bend to pick up my jeans and the vibrating phone. I've got twenty-five minutes to get ready for work, the screen says. My heart sinks at the time and I look up to see Jack stretching out in bed, one hand resting behind his head. His beautiful chest is on show, a landscape of abs on full display. It takes all my self-restraint not to crawl back under the covers with him.

He winks at me and my knees just about buckle.

"Good morning, beautiful."

The words make my heart flutter. I tuck my hair behind an ear with a shy smile.

"I need to get ready for work."

Jack hums happily as he crawls out of bed and grabs my hips. "Good idea, let's take a shower."

Before I can protest, he picks me up and carries me into the bathroom.

"Be a good girl and let me see you," he growls into my neck, tearing the sarong-sheet from my body. I am weak to that growl. There is no resisting him now.

By the time he's done with me, I'm leaving the bathroom with wobbly legs. It takes everything in me not to fall over.

"I've got to teach my class today, and I can barely walk," I grumble as I towel off and get dressed for the day. Jack swaggers back into the room, naked and dewy from the shower. He moves with confidence and gives me a devilish grin.

"I'm sorry… But I'm not sorry."

When we're both dressed, we come together in a warm embrace, arms wrapped around each other and eyes sparkling. I plant another kiss on his lips.

"I have no regrets," I whisper, before kissing him again.

Jack's hands flex on my waist and he buries his face in my neck for a moment. "Good. Me neither."

I float into work.

Last night, I followed my heart, and it led me right back to Jack.

We are hopelessly and utterly in love, and nothing can go wrong.

That is exactly what is running through my mind when I enter my classroom to discover Beverly and Mr. Hargreaves standing at the front like a pair of undercover police officers.

I hold my breath and force a smile. "Morning!" I say. I'm trying my hardest to appear pleasantly surprised by this anything-but-pleasant surprise.

"Miss Scott, will you accompany me to my office please?" Principal Hart says. She nods to Mr. Hargreaves. "Vice Principal Hargreaves will cover your class."

The long walk to her office is like walking the plank off a pirate ship. I knew there would be a price for my happiness. It's time to pay.

But I don't care what she can do to me. Being with Jack is worth whatever drama and suffering she plans to throw at me.

"Take a seat," Principal Hart says, motioning to the moth-eaten chair in front of her desk. I perch on the edge and try to ignore the way my body is throbbing—an echo of Jack's love.

Gosh, that man knows how to worship a body.

"I've been informed you are in a relationship with one of the parents," Principal Hart says, snapping me out of my thoughts. I clear my throat.

We sit across from each other, sizing ourselves up. The two women in Jack's life.

I try not to picture Jack kissing her. Even though I know that once upon a time, he must have touched her too. Many times.

I swallow against my rising nausea as the Principal blinks at me. "Don't worry, I'm not going to fire you," she says, looking at me with satisfaction. I'm surprised.

Then the thought hits me.

She doesn't *need* to fire me.

Seeing Jack's ex-wife every day, constantly reminded of her existence and taunted by the fact that she was once ravished by him, is a fresh kind of torture that I'm not sure I can stomach for a day. Let alone my whole career.

In case that's not enough to crumble my resolve, Principal Hart leans forward and plants a cold smile on her face. "Every class you teach, I'll be watching you. Every time you so much as look in my son's direction, I'll be there. The second you put a toe out of line, I'm filing a report. And I'll keep filing reports until I fill up a ring binder. Then I'm going to destroy you. And you will never be able to work in another school, ever again. In fact, by the time I'm done with you, Miss Scott, no one will touch you with a ten-foot pole. Not even the cleaning company assigned to work at Taco Bell."

I grind my teeth, chewing on the threat.

If there is one thing I know about myself, it's that I'm a free bird.

If someone threatens to trap me in a cage, or take away my ability to choose, I'll do whatever it takes to escape. My blood runs cold as she stares me down.

Despite the tornado of fury raging inside me, my voice is surprisingly calm when I reply,

"That's fine. I quit anyway."

Principal Hart leans back in her chair, her expression neutral. I can't decide if she was expecting this move or not. The corner of her mouth twitches like she's thinking about smiling, she seems to decide against it at the very last minute.

"How does it feel?" she asks.

"What?"

She leans forward again. "Knowing that you are solely responsible for hurting an entire family."

She laces her fingers together and rests her hands on the desk. "You hurt me when I was at my lowest. I was caring for my dad after his hip replacement surgery while you snuck around with my ex-husband right in front of my son."

I open my mouth but shut it when she raises a palm to show she isn't done.

"You've hurt Jack, because I simply refuse to let him see Brodie while he's with you. And you're hurting Brodie because—for reasons beyond my comprehension—he likes having you as his teacher. Now he's going to be left with Mr. Hargreaves, who we all know is about as energetic as a stapler."

I wring my hands as I think about it.

But then Jack's words echo in my mind. "You can't keep Brodie from seeing his father, he'll fight you in court."

Principal Hart smirks. She looks far too smug in her fancy, white, button up blouse, her perfectly tamed hair pinned back. Her features are severe; She's wearing heavier make up than usual. I wonder if she did that on purpose. To assert dominance.

The thought amuses me. I straighten my spine and roll my shoulders back in defense.

She gives me a smile so sharp, it makes me recoil again. "You're a silly girl, aren't you?" she says, in a sickly-sweet voice. "I *can* stop him from seeing Brodie. And sure, he can take me to court. But do you know how long those legal proceedings take? Months. Sometimes years, if you get a good lawyer who knows how to slow down the process." She gives me a look, her eyes flashing dangerously. "Meanwhile, Brodie is growing up thinking his dad doesn't care about him."

I screw up my face in disgust. "You would

put your son through that?" I can hardly believe the thought. "Don't you care what's best for Brodie?"

Principal Hart's fist slams down on the desk as her smile dissipates. "Don't you *dare* ask me that. You think I don't lay awake at night obsessing over what's best for my son? Do you have any idea what kind of nightmares I've been through ever since he was born?"

She rises to a stand and sucks in a deep breath, as though to control her temper. "Maybe you should know that your dearest Jack is only caring and attentive to you because he has literally nothing else to do with his time right now. You know he killed a patient, right?"

I jump to my feet, my blood boiling. "And why did he do that? Because he saw you cheating on him!"

We stare at each other in angry silence, both breathing heavily. Then Principal Hart lifts her brows and turns her back to me to look out of the windows overlooking the empty playground.

"I'll make you a deal, Miss Scott."

I hold my breath. I never expected to be offered a deal.

My instincts, however, are telling me that

anything the Principal has to offer me will come at a great cost.

"I need to know first…" She turns around to give me a steely look. "Do you love Jack?"

I don't hesitate to nod. She eyes me closely, as if she's a human lie detector. I must have passed the test because she nods back.

"If you truly love Jack… And you care about what's best for my son…" she pauses for effect. "You will disappear."

I open my mouth in shock. "Excuse me?"

Principal Hart tilts her head to look at me with pity. Like she's about to make a move and announce Checkmate. "You will disappear."

"But I already quit… What more do you…?" I begin, but I shut my mouth at the sight of the woman's wicked smile. She is pure evil.

"You want me to stop seeing Jack," I say, my voice sounding flat.

"Ah. You're not completely stupid, I see," she says, straightening up and beaming with satisfaction. "Here's the deal: you disappear. I'll pay your wages for two weeks to help you find another job, and I'll even give a glowing reference to any prospective boss that calls my number. Which I think is extremely generous considering the circumstances..." She studies her fingernails in the sunlight and hums to herself. "With you out of the picture, I will be more than happy to arrange for my son to stay with his dad on a regular basis. It's a win-win for everyone, don't you think?"

I am numb.

She's offering me an olive branch by not totally throwing me under the bus. I can get another job in a school without my reputation being completely destroyed.

But I'll never see Brodie or Jack again.

Ever.

That is one heck of a price for so-called happiness.

My eyes prickle, and there's a sharp itch in the back of my throat when I swallow. The principal studies me and leans forward. "If you truly care about them, you will do this. To stay is the most selfish thing you can do. Hasn't Jack been through enough legal drama this year? And hasn't Brodie suffered enough with his parents' divorce?"

I open and close my mouth several times while I think on it.

My body is still humming from the toe-curling night I spent with the man who I'm sure is Mr.

Right. Now I'm expected to just walk away and never see him again?

"What do I tell Jack?" I ask myself aloud. The principal gives me a sharp look.

"You tell him you've had a change of heart. That you are leaving and never want to see him again. When he tries to talk to you, you don't pick up the phone. You pass go; you don't meet him at the door. You *disappear*, Miss Scott." She slams her hand on the table again. "You disappear, or the deal is off."

My heart is splintering as I look at the triumphant smile on the Principal's face. She knows she's got me.

Jack can fight her, but she'll drag it out for as long as possible. Brodie won't get to see him the entire time, and I can't bear to put them both through that kind of agony.

I won't stand between Brodie and his dad. No matter how much it destroys me.

"Okay," I say, nearly choking on the word.

The principal lifts a hand to her ear. "Okay, what? Tell me."

I blink away tears to clear my vision and give her a resolute look, my heart shattering into millions of fragments. "I will disappear."

22

JACK

After changing my clothes back in my apartment, I clean up the place while I hum to myself. Even after a shower, I can still smell Chessy all over me.

My hands flex at the thought of holding her again, and my heart swells when I picture her coming back from work.

After spending an explosive night with her—and a quick refresher this morning—I am convinced there is nothing that can stand in the way of our happiness. As long as we have each other, the world can be full of bitter Beverlys for all I care.

Chessy is The One.

I'll never stop thinking of ways to show her

just how much she means to me.

In my mission to getting my life back together, I call Charles, the Chief of Surgery, and ask to come into the hospital for a chat. To my relief, he tells me to swing by at lunch.

"It's good to see you looking so much better," he says after I walk into his office.

I can't stop smiling as I sit in the chair and take in the familiar surroundings. The smell of antiseptic cleaner sparks old memories of days when I was on top of the world, performing surgery after surgery. Meeting patients. Doing consults. Saving lives, one day at a time.

Now that I have my life in order, I'm ready to cut again.

"I've been speaking to a shrink, taking care of myself," I scrub my face in thought, trying to avoid bringing up the fact that I've been sleeping with the cute neighbor. Truth is, that's got more to do with my elevated mood than anything else.

Charles hums. "And when do you think you'll be ready to come back?"

"Tomorrow," I say, holding his gaze. I refuse to blink, showing how serious I am. Charles studies me carefully for a few moments, then finally gives a curt nod of approval. "Great. I'll inform the director."

ON THE WAY HOME, I PICK UP A POSY OF RED roses and grab a bag of chocolate fudge squares from Elle's Kitchen, Chessy's favorite bakery. The world is brighter now as I waltz down the city streets. If it starts to rain, I'll dance in the puddles and swing around the streetlamps. Nothing can put me down.

My feet are floating and it's as though I'm walking on clouds through the throng of grumpy commuters.

Someone bumps into my shoulder, but it fails to wipe the goofy smile off my face.

I linger outside a jewelry store and eye up the sparkling diamond rings on display.

Suddenly, Chessy's idea to get married doesn't sound so bad.

It's like the old saying—when you know, you know. Besides, Chessy was right. Marrying her would take away Beverly's power. I enter the store grinning from ear to ear.

I expect Beverly is giving Chessy a hard time

at the school, but Chessy knows the plan. I'm certain she won't be rattled. In any case, I'll dedicate the rest of the night to making her forget all about the stress of the day. I'll start kissing her neck and work my way down, relishing the joy of every sweet inch of her squeezable, delicious body until she begs me to stop.

My mouth waters at the thought.

I crave her touch. Her hand fits so nicely in mine, and I love the way her shapely body fits snug against me. Laying with her feels like home.

She grounds me and elevates me all at the same time.

I'm intoxicated by her love, and yet I've never had so much clarity.

I pace around my apartment, waiting for her to text or call. The hours tick by and the sun begins to descend, and my heartbeat picks up speed.

"Just calling to see how it went today. Love you," I say, leaving a message for the tenth time.

Another hour rolls by and I open my door to look down the empty hall. I frown and call her again. It goes straight to voice mail.

"Hope you're okay. I expected you back by now. Call me when you get this."

At ten p.m. the hairs on the back of my neck are standing on end.

Something is not right.

Just then, I hear footsteps in the hall. I wrench the door open, flooded with relief, but my eyes land on the last person I expect to see; Wyatt.

He gives me a sheepish smile. "Sorry, she's not here," he says, reading my mind. Then he avoids making eye contact altogether.

"What happened? Is she okay?" I ask, walking out into the hall.

The squeal of door hinges behind me tells me Bob from next door has popped his head out to be nosey. I resist the urge to look back.

Wyatt shrugs. "She doesn't want to see you anymore."

His frank delivery is like a smack to the face. "What do you mean?"

Wyatt fiddles with a chain of keys and unlocks the door. Then he gives me a look of pity. "She asked me to get her stuff."

I start to pace the hall, panicking. "What!"

Wyatt walks into her apartment and I follow him inside before he can shut the door in my face. This must be a mistake. Chessy was happy and content when she left for work this morning, I made sure of that.

She said she had no regrets.

I pull out my phone and try to call her again, but Wyatt gives me a disapproving stare. "Don't waste your time, she's not taking your calls."

I look at him with horror. "Why?"

"She doesn't need the drama," he says, looking around the apartment with a sigh.

"But why would she just leave without talking to me?" I wonder aloud.

Wyatt leans forward to look me in the eye, then utters three words that freeze my heart.

"Ask your ex-wife."

***

"DAD!" BRODIE THROWS HIMSELF ROUND MY middle as soon as the door to my old house opens.

Beverly is standing in the background in a bathrobe, her hair in a fluffy towel.

"What are you doing up so late, buddy?" I ask, ruffling his hair.

Beverly waves the question aside. "Oh, we were celebrating. Isn't that right, kiddo?" she says, her cheeks rosy. Brodie zooms around in circles in excitement and begins to talk a million miles an hour, as always.

"Mom is taking me to Disneyland tomorrow."

I pinch my brows in confusion. "But it's a school day."

Brodie stops running and hops up and down with glee. "We're taking it off!"

I drag a hand through my hair and fake a smile while Brodie runs down the hall to his room. I shoot Beverly a glare.

"What did you say to Chessy?"

Beverly crosses her arms and lifts her brows in suspicion. "She quit this morning and I said I would give her a glowing reference. In spite of all this scandal, she's a proficient teacher. And I can be a mature adult, regardless of how you see me."

My mind is reeling. "That doesn't explain why she won't pick up my calls."

Beverly shrugs. "You think that's my problem? Whatever is going on between you two is none of my business. It's like you said…" She takes a few steps closer to me and prods my shoulder with a bony finger. "I can't tell you who you can and cannot date."

I clench my jaw and take a step back so she can't touch me again. "What did you do?"

Beverly doesn't bristle under my accusatory stare. She just shrugs. "Nothing, I swear. And to show you how mature I can be, I want you to know that I'm happy to continue our prior arrangement. You have Brodie two weekends a month, if that's all right with you?"

I freeze.

"You'll let me see Brodie?"

My instincts are screaming danger at me. Something happened today, and Chessy's silence is maddening. But I can't stop a glimmer of happiness from rising to the surface as I see Brodie running back down the hall with his arms laden in toys.

"Look what Mom bought me," he says, laying them out.

Beverly watches on with a placid smile on her face as Brodie shows me all the new dinosaurs he's added to his collection. I make fake noises of amazement, but my mind is miles away.

Chessy is gone. I get to see Brodie without a fight.

My heart swings on a pendulum between joy and sorrow.

When Brodie hurries down the hall to collect more toys, I whisper to Beverly.

"Did you tell Chessy to leave me?"

Beverly looks at me with pure disdain. "How dare you think I'd stoop so low," she spits as if the words are poison. "Whatever's going on between you and her has nothing to do with me."

"But we…" I trail off, scratching the back of my neck while flashes of last night cross my mind. Beverly laughs. "Has it never occurred to you, that you maybe have more baggage than she's willing to handle?"

The words sting. I stare at her, hoping with every fiber of my being that she's wrong.

A small part of my mind can't help believing her, though.

What if Chessy did decide that I come with too much baggage?

Isn't that what Wyatt said too?

Knowing that Beverly isn't going to divulge any more information, I give up. "Well… Okay then," I say, forcing myself to sound bewildered and not completely destroyed by the news. "I'll be working at the hospital this weekend, so I'll take Brodie next week."

Beverly nods. "I'm glad you're going back to work. Fixing broken hearts is what you do best."

She's either horribly mistaken, or she's being facetious.

Because all I seem to do these days is break hearts. Especially my own.

IT'S ALMOST MIDNIGHT WHEN I SHOW UP OUTSIDE Blaze and Leila's mansion. I should go to bed for my first day back at work tomorrow, but my soul will not rest until I know what I did wrong.

Chessy can't just shut me out of her life with no warning and not even a goodbye.

I hammer my fist on the front door and wait for several minutes, listening to the deafening sound of crickets. When no one comes to the door, I bang against it several more times.

Suddenly, the lock clicks and the door opens with a squeal. The moon illuminates Lucy's pale face as she squints at me. "What the heck are you doing here this late?" she asks. "You know we thought you were an axe murderer?"

I give her a look. "Do you always open the door to people you think are axe murderers?"

Lucy blinks, looking unimpressed. I rest a hand on the doorframe and nudge my foot in the opening just in case she thinks about slamming it on me. "Is she here?" I ask, my heart thrumming my ribcage.

Lucy's nostril's flare and her pupils dilate.

I'll take that as a yes.

"Can I speak to her?" I ask.

Lucy shakes her head. "Absolutely not."

I drop my hand, a lump in my throat. "So, what? I'm supposed to just forget about her? Just like that?" I snap my fingers.

Lucy nods. "It's for the best."

I rest a hand on my aching heart. "But I love her. And I thought she loved me too."

Lucy nips her bottom lip, wrapping her robe around her more tightly. Then she leans in to murmur something to me. I have to edge closer to catch her words.

"Sometimes, we have to let people go. *Because* we love them."

She gives me an intense stare, as though she's trying to beam information to me using telepathy. My shoulders sag as I step back and nod. "Okay. Fine. If that's what she wants."

The chill in the air coats my soul in ice and I feel myself go totally numb. "Tell her…" I draw a blank. I don't know what to tell her. How am I supposed to let her go? How is that showing someone you love them?

But I'm out of options. I swallow and take a few more steps. "Tell her to have a happy life."

Lucy's eyes grow misty and she nods, then shuts the door.

I turn around and walk back to my car, falling apart inside.

23

CHESSY

It's the day of Lucy and Wyatt's wedding and the weather could not be more perfect. The leaves are a beautiful blend of chestnut brown and burnt orange, and the golden sun is casting a warm glow over the gardens. The scene is rich in colors of green, red, and gold.

I continue to stare out of the long window from my room in Leila's house, watching the service staff setting up the white gazebo. Another group is dressing the rows of chairs in white organza.

There's a floral arch at the front where the priest will stand with Lucy and Wyatt. That's where they'll exchange their vows.

I clutch the towel around me, sighing as I

wonder how I'm going to get through the day without bursting into fits of tears.

It's been less than a week since I ghosted Jack.

Less than a week, but it seems like ten years.

In many ways, I'm glad we were able to spend one amazing night together. But in other ways, I'm kicking myself with regret. Experiencing the full extent of Jack's love has ruined me forever.

No man will ever measure up.

No one will be so in tune with my needs. I tremble at the memory of the way his strong hands lifted me up so easily. He dominated me in the most delightful, beautiful way.

He explored me like an adventurer—cheeky, daring, fearless.

I explored him with joy.

We were vulnerable. In body *and* soul.

But I had to let him go.

I look up at the fluffy white clouds in the sky and shake my fist at the heavens. How can the universe send me The One and let him sweep me off my feet, only to send me crashing down to earth with a big bump?

The One turned out to be Mr. Wrong Timing, and I'm not sure what's more painful; to go your whole life never finding him, or to find him and not be able to be with him.

The only silver lining I can take from all of this is that he taught me the difference between lust and love.

Lust is desiring someone's body. Love is cherishing body and soul.

The connection we had was like nothing I've ever known before. We became so in sync with each other. His scent would soothe me after a long day as I curled up in his arms each night.

I fell in love with the sound of his deep rumbling voice. He could have talked to me about surgeries for hours and I'd have listened with my eyes half-closed, just basking in his warmth.

He was my home, my rock. My everything.

Now, Wyatt and Lucy are going to get married —Leila has given me the responsibility to oversee the wedding arrangements—and I'm reminded of Jack at every turn.

This should be our happy ending too. I truly thought this was going to be my fairy tale story.

But perhaps I'm cursed to always fall for the wrong guy.

I'll be like Joey from *Friends*; watching

everyone I love find their soul mate while I remain single forever.

Single and alone.

After leaving my job, I moved in with Leila, who took great delight in bossing me around every ten minutes. She's a million times more needy now that Blaze is on tour.

I've spent evenings rubbing her swollen feet, bringing her drinks, going over every minute wedding detail. Everything from the appetizers and musical pieces to the color of bobby pins we'll put in our hair. Lucy shot that one down later, though, saying bobby pins come straight out of Satan's toolkit and are thereby banned from her wedding.

Which reminds me. I've been breaking up more than a few arguments between my older sisters.

I pull on my dress and comb my hair in a hurry. I don't pay too much attention as I apply a natural make up look, then I slip into my white sandals and leave the room, drawn to the sound of Leila's wails.

"What's wrong?" I say, with an eye roll. Leila has been a lot more emotional lately.

Two nights ago, she cried during a life insurance commercial. Yesterday she cried at an empty cup.

An empty cup.

I just stared at the thing, laying on the ground on its side with not so much as a single drop left in it, and all I could think about was how much I related to that dang cup. I have nothing left in me either.

I walk into Leila's room and gasp at the sight.

Leila is in her lilac gown, looking at her reflection in the full-length mirror on the wall and sobbing.

Big fat tears roll down her cheeks, making black lines down her face.

"Look at my legs!" she wails, pointing.

I was too busy looking at her bump, which looks bigger than ever. It's made the dress even shorter, stopping it just above the knee. Her legs are usually slender, but they've ballooned like two big, over-stuffed sausages.

"What happened?" I ask in alarm, stepping forward to take a closer look.

Leila sobs even harder as she plonks down on the side of the bed. "I can't walk without getting out of breath. I feel sick all the time, and now I look ugly too."

"You don't look ugly," I argue, picking up a wet wipe to remove the mascara lines from her cheeks. I can't argue against the rest of her complaints. Pregnancy has been hard on her.

"I look like Princess Fiona," Leila moans, hiccupping. "Lucy is getting married in an hour and Blaze is still away and I'm just fat, ugly, and alone."

She wails again and I rub her back with a soothing hum. "You look beautiful, Leila. Blaze will be home before you know it, and you'll get to see Lucy and Wyatt get married in your gorgeous garden. Just like you wanted."

I give her my signature Chessy look. The one that says everything is fine. *Stay positive.*

But my heart is heavy.

I glance at her legs again. The skin is blotchy, and I make a mental note to google that later. Surely, this isn't normal, even during pregnancy?

"What's happened to your legs?"

We both look up at the sound of Lucy's voice and gasp in unison. Lucy is in the doorway, already wearing her wedding gown. It's got a lace fitted bodice and fans out in a full circle of white satin material to the floor. Her hair falls in soft waves to her shoulders with one section tucked behind an ear.

"Lucy, you look…"

"Prettier than Galadriel," Leila finishes for me, putting on her brave big sister face and reaching out for Lucy. Lucy steps forward and they hug. I wrap them both up in my arms too.

When we break apart, Leila's got tears in her eyes again. "I'm sorry," she says with a sniff. "It's your day and I really want it to be perfect. But I'm… Not feeling good."

Lucy and I exchange worried looks. "Do you need us to call a doctor?"

Leila shakes her head. "I'll call in the morning. I just wish I could do something. I never knew pregnancy could be so debilitating."

Lucy frowns at me with concern, then looks back at Leila. "I'm worried about you. I don't think this is normal."

Leila gives us both a hard look and dabs her eyes with a tissue. "Stop looking at me like that. I'm fine. I just… Let's get you married."

A string quartet plays Canon in D while Lucy walks alone down the aisle. She's clutching a simple bouquet of white roses and lilies, and smiles shyly as she approaches Wyatt.

I'm standing up at the front, wondering who half of the guests are. I've never seen them before in my life. Our mom isn't here, and my annoyance at her keeps rising. I try to suppress it.

I tried to call her, but she wouldn't pick up, so I texted her the details instead.

I can see that she read the message, and even though she never replied, part of me is hoping she'll show up at the last minute.

Wyatt is all smiles as he watches Lucy walk to him, and he leans over to mutter something in my ear. I don't quite catch his words; my heartbeat is like a marching battalion headed for war. I give him a nod and a smile anyway.

Then I step back and try to ignore the lump in my throat while Wyatt and Lucy exchange their vows. Every few seconds, I glance over at Leila in the front row. Her chest is heaving visibly as though she's run a marathon.

Worry tugs at my mouth and pulls it down into a frown. But the priest announces the bride and groom as husband and wife just then and I have to force a smile.

Wyatt plants the sweetest kiss on Lucy's lips. Everyone breaks out in applause. She chuckles, wraps her arms around his neck, and dives in for a stronger one.

A wave of laughter and applause ripples through the guests.

Later, I listen to Wyatt's parents toast and the happy laughter that follows. One of Lucy's co-workers cracks a few jokes, and finally, Leila wobbles to her feet. Her face is clammy and she's breathless, but she dabs her face with a napkin and raises her glass.

Everyone falls silent and watches. Smiles falter and there are whispers flying around the gazebo. Worried expressions are unmistakable.

"I've never seen a couple more perfect for each other," she begins. She takes a few short breaths, beaming at Wyatt and Lucy, who smile back at her. Those two seem to be in their own happy bubble. She clears her throat. "When I first met Wyatt, I—"

Bang.

Everyone jumps to their feet and my heart stops as I register what just happened.

"We need a doctor! Somebody call 9-1-1," Wyatt shouts as everyone crowds the table.

Leila is on the floor. I pick up her wrist. "She's got a pulse, but her fingernails are blue.

That's a bad sign, right?" I ask the people around me.

A sea of wide eyes stare at me, but no one moves. I realize then that bystander apathy is real, and no one is going to rush to help me, so I take matters into my own hands.

"Lucy, call Blaze. Wyatt, help me pick her up."

Wyatt and I grunt as we lift Leila's limp body and carry her across the gardens to the line of parked cars out front. "I know it's your wedding day, but can you take us to the hospital?" I ask him.

Wyatt nods. "Of course. My car is right over there."

We bundle Leila in the back of his Audi, and Lucy climbs in with us. "Is she breathing? Did you check her airways?" she asks. Wyatt pulls out of the drive.

The engine roars to life as the car navigates traffic with ease. I cradle Leila's head in my lap. My hands are clammy and a sense of panic is now flooding my body, gripping my heart in a vice.

I bite my tongue hard to stop the tears in my eyes from falling.

Don't cry. Don't cry. Don't cry.

All three of us carry Leila in through the hospital doors, where a nurse dashes toward us. Somebody mutters as we pass by. "Isn't that Blaze Hopkin's wife?"

I'm too caught up in the madness of the moment to remember that Leila can't leave her house without paparazzi following her every move. One of the downfalls of being married to an A-list celebrity is the endless scrutiny. It's why she rarely leaves the house on the best of days.

"What happened?" the nurse asks as she grabs a stretcher and helps us lay Leila on it.

"She's pregnant with twins and she fainted," I say. My hands won't stop shaking so I cross my arms to still them. "She was saying she didn't feel good earlier."

"How long have her legs been this swollen?" the nurse asks. Lucy and I look at each other.

I think back about her swollen feet and ankles; I watched them grow as the week went on, but ballooned like this? "A day," I say firmly. "She's been complaining a lot about her ankles being swollen this week, but today is the first time she's been upset about her legs."

The next thing I know, there's a team of

people in white lab coats flooding the scene. Then we're bombarded with instructions.

"We'll take her from here. Have a seat. Somebody will be out with an update."

Then they start talking to each other at top speed, speaking in medical jargon that makes zero sense to me.

Shaken and nauseated, I follow Wyatt and Lucy to a group of empty chairs in the waiting room. We sit in a huddle. All three of us are ashen faced and wide-eyed.

Wyatt and Lucy stand out like sore thumbs in their wedding clothes. The people around us begin to stare.

Minutes pass like hours. Hours pass like days. We wait. And wait. And wait.

We take turns to approach the front desk for an update, but each time, we're told the same thing. "No news yet," the nurse tells us. "The doctors will see you shortly."

All sorts of terrible scenarios start to play out in my head. After I watch the third hour pass by, I begin to silently pray to God. I hope someone is there to hear my prayer.

Please. Please, don't take my sister or her babies. I'll do anything. Anything. I'll spend the rest of my life a spinster if that's what you want. I'll take care of her. I'll…

A bubble of emotion rises to my chest. I have to stop and sniff to keep myself from falling apart.

The doors fly open then, and Blaze charges into the hospital with a blinding barrage of camera flashes behind him. His sharp eyes take in the room and lock with mine. The look of devastation on my face must be plain. He makes a beeline for the front desk.

His fist comes down on the counter so hard the nurse at the front desk jumps. "I'm here for Leila Hopkins. Tell me what's wrong with my wife."

I want to tell him it's no use. Lucy and I have been up and down multiple times asking for updates. No one seems to know anything.

But after a few minutes of heated discussion, a door opens and an impossibly thin man in a black suit walks out. He stretches out a hand. "Blaze Hopkins, my name is Walter Herring. I am the Director of this hospital, and I'm happy to help you."

I marvel at the way the staff completely transforms around Blaze. I guess this is the treatment you get when you're a billionaire. I dash to Blaze's side along with Lucy and Wyatt, while Mr. Herring gives some information.

"Your wife has congenital heart disease; we suspect she was born with it. I'm surprised it has never been picked up in her medical exams…"

Lucy and I stare at each other, stunned. Our mom never so much as took us to the doctor, let alone the hospital. And all this time, Leila had a heart condition.

Mr. Herring clears his throat. "Her oxygen stats dropped to 75%, so we had to deliver the babies via c-section."

Blaze closes his eyes and rests a hand on his forehead. His face is pale now. "The babies…"

"They're both in the neo-natal unit. You will be able to see them shortly."

Blaze looks up. "They're okay?" he asks in a breathless voice. "And Leila? She's going to be okay?"

Mr. Herring swallows and nods to another man in a white lab coat. This one dashes forward.

"Mr. Hopkins, I'm Charles Green. Chief of Surgery."

Blaze takes a deep breath, looking from the Director to the surgeon with his lips pursed. I can see the cogs spinning in his mind, but he's too paralyzed by the situation to speak. I take over.

"Is Leila's heart okay?"

Dr. Green looks at me, then around at all of us, before he finally turns to Blaze and places a hand on his shoulder. My stomach knots. That's never a good sign.

Please, no. God, please don't take my sister.

"Because her condition was never picked up and monitored, she has unfortunately developed a rare complication."

Blaze's eyes are glassy. His Adam's apple bobs. "What does that mean?"

All of us hold hands, bracing for the news.

"It's called aortic dissection. There is a slight tear in the main artery, and it requires immediate surgery."

Blaze nods so fast his neck cricks. "Right. Right. So, that's happening now, is it?"

"She is being prepped for surgery as we speak."

"Can I see her?" Blaze asks, the strength in his voice fading.

Dr. Green shakes his head.

"I'm afraid not. We need to get her into surgery immediately."

Blaze grabs the doctor's coat in a fist and pulls the man close to glower at him. "You get the best surgeon there is, do you understand me? You have no idea how precious that heart is."

The surrounding doctors flinch and some take a step forward, as though thinking about whether to intervene. The Chief of Surgery motions for them to back down. He remains totally calm in the face of Blaze's fury and nods.

"I assure you, Mr. Hopkins, that we have the best surgeon on the East Coast. Doctor Hart is getting ready to perform surgery right now."

Blaze lets go of the doctor and we all take a breath. Then Blaze, Wyatt, and Lucy turn to look at me with stunned eyes. We all know the surgeon he's referring to.

Jack.

The silver lining of working at the hospital is that I've been able to bury myself in work all week. I've consulted, briefed, and even assisted some surgeries.

It's been a pleasant escape.

In fact, I actually began to think my PTSD was cured.

The other surgeons told me their war stories of the first time a patient died on their operating table. They all said getting back on the horse—or picking up the scalpel, as they liked to call it—was their cure.

And they were right. The more patients that came and went, the more confident I was in my abilities again.

Until tonight.

I walked into the room, picked up the tablet to read the patient information, and felt an iron band wrap itself around my chest when I registered the patient's name.

Leila Hopkins. Chessy's pregnant older sister.

She was in a bad state when I walked into the room—unconscious and hooked up to life support.

Her legs were swollen to the point that her skin had grown taut.

I read her file in disbelief. Undiagnosed congenital heart disease leading to aortic dissection.

How could this happen?

The other doctors began to fill me in on her stats and my brain kicked into overdrive.

The poor woman had been through an emergency c-section and was clinging to life. I booked an operating room and sent her to surgery within minutes.

As I scrubbed in and prepped for surgery, I told myself to stay calm.

This is just a normal patient and an easy dissection repair.

I almost didn't walk up to the table.

There's a conflict of interest. It should be someone else doing this.

One of the nurses puts a hand on my shoulder and her kind eyes encourage me.

I walk up to Leila, and we begin.

I put the scalpel on her skin and press.

I try not to think about who the patient is as I open her up.

But then her beating heart is front of me, bleeding all over my hands… I'm transported back in time.

It's just like the day my life turned upside down.

It wasn't my fault. This wasn't my fault.

If I don't perform the repair quickly, Leila will follow the same fate as the patient who sent me into a spiral of depression.

I shut my eyes for a splinter of a second and send a silent prayer to whatever deity is out there to listen.

Then Chessy's face floods my mind and I take a long, deep breath, picturing her sunny smile as we walked with Brodie through Central Park. I listen to the echo of her laughter in my mind and see the sparkle of her pretty eyes… The warmth of her hand in mine.

I set to work.

I am not a religious man, but I can swear that something is guiding my hands, helping me with every stitch. The other surgeons and nurses perform their respective task with zero mistakes. We work together like a well-oiled machine, tackling each problem as they arise.

When the heart goes into failure, panic doesn't take me. It's just another problem. Hours pass like seconds, and the next thing I know, I'm sewing her up to the beautiful sound of a steady heartbeat.

"Congratulations, Dr. Hart. That was miraculous," the anesthetist says.

"Well done, Jack. Nice work."

I look up at the sound of the intercom in a slight daze. Charles is watching from the observatory room. A mixture of pride and intense relief washes over me.

I nod to everyone, thanking them for their assistance.

I manage to hold it together with my head held high, all the way into the other room, before I break down at the sink.

THE NEXT DAY, I WALK INTO LEILA'S HOSPITAL room to find her propped up in bed, surrounded by her family. Everyone turns to me as I enter. I try to keep a straight face.

Leila looks at me like she's a kid and I'm Santa. "You saved my life!"

I let a smile take over as I take her outstretched hand. "How are you feeling now?"

She nods to her legs under the covers and wriggles them. "The swelling has gone down, thank goodness. And I don't feel so breathless anymore."

"Good," I say, picking up her chart. There's a flash of movement in my peripheral vision, but I resist the urge to look. I know it's Chessy. She's here somewhere in the crowd of family.

I can't bring myself to look at her.

The room whirls suddenly, and I find my face in one of Blaze's pectorals. He's pulled me in for a tight hug. "I can't begin to tell you how grateful I am for what you've done," he says hoarsely. We break apart and his eyes twinkle as he gives my hand a hearty shake.

I nod to him. "How are the babies?"

Blaze takes out his phone to show me pictures. "They're tiny, but strong. A boy and a girl."

I clap him on the shoulder. "Congratulations, Dad. Welcome to the club. You will never stop worrying about them or get a good night's sleep again."

Blaze chuckles. I crane my neck around to look at Leila again. "We need to keep an eye on that heart of yours from now on. Take good care of yourself, all right?"

Leila nods in understanding. There's another movement and a few whispers, but I clench my jaw, determined to ignore it. Then I turn and leave the room without a single glance back.

As I walk away, I consider turning around again to look for Chessy in the crowded room. To touch her hands... Pull her close and feel her body against mine... To lift her face and kiss her lips.

But she left for a reason. I have to respect that.

If I take one look at her, I know I will fall to my knees and weep at her feet, begging her to take me back.

I can't maintain a civil conversation with her, and I'd rather not make a fool of myself in front of her entire family.

I keep walking.

My chest throbs and I grind my teeth, cursing

the fact that some hearts can't be so easily repaired.

CHESSY

The room falls silent when the door swings shut behind Jack.

Then everyone turns to look at me.

"Why didn't you say anything?" Lucy asks from Wyatt's lap.

It's pretty obvious that after Leila's surgery, Lucy and Wyatt spent all morning making up for lost time. They've pretty much started their honeymoon.

He can't keep his hands off her, and her cheeks are flushed.

I'm happy for them. Most of all, I'm beyond relieved that my baby niece and nephew are okay, and that Leila is still with us.

On the other hand, my emotions are all over

the place. I wanted to thank Jack for saving my sister. I moved, hoping he would look my way and prompt me to speak.

But he didn't so much as glance in my direction.

Beneath the courtesy, I could see the hurt on his face. My insides are squirming at the knowledge that I did that to him.

"I just can't…" I say, thinking about Beverly's threat. "You know why."

There's a heavy silence, then Blaze and Wyatt look at each other as though they're having a silent conversation. "Why don't we get these girls a cup of coffee?" Blaze offers, giving Wyatt a pointed look. Wyatt seems to get the message and nods back.

Lucy grumbles in protest when he lifts her from his lap. He bends to give her a kiss, then joins Blaze by the door. "We'll be back."

When the door shuts behind them, Lucy and I crawl onto the hospital bed to snuggle Leila.

Now alone, our emotions bubble over the surface. All of the shock, worry, and horror comes out in violent sobs.

Leila wraps us up in her arms while we cry.

"Don't *ever* scare us like that again," I say, squeezing her hand.

"You're not allowed to die. Ever. Okay?" Lucy adds, sniffing.

Leila kisses the top of our heads and squeezes us tight. "Remember when Mom left us? I promised I would take care of you. I'll always keep that promise."

The memory hits me like a jack hammer to the chest.

I never consciously thought about how my mom's abandonment might have affected me, but it was the ultimate rejection. Who gets dumped by their own mom?

Maybe that's why I've always clung to my sisters, and I'm always falling for the wrong guy.

I hate being alone. And being left behind is so much worse.

Now that I think about it, is that why I took Beverly's deal? I took matters in my own hands, and I thought I was doing it for Jack and Brodie's best interest.

Lucy lifts her head. "Speaking of Mom, have you heard from her?"

I wipe my eyes. "I sent her a text last night telling her what happened, so she knows."

Lucy nods. "Even if she missed it, you and Blaze are all over the tabloids. She can't miss that."

Leila sighs heavily and looks out at the window with a vacant look on her face. "She sent me a text message saying she hopes all is well with the babies, but she's not coming. She had the cheek to sign off as *Grandma*."

Lucy and I exchange looks of disgust. How could she not come when Leila was practically on her deathbed? The three of us hold each other again and cry quietly.

"Promise me we'll always be there for each other," Leila says, her voice flooded with emotion.

"Always," Lucy and I say in unison.

When we break apart, Leila looks down at me with a motherly smile. She smooths my hair, then gives me a pointed look. "Now, what are we going to do about you?"

I frown. "What do you mean?"

"Didn't you feel the tension when he was in the room? It was palpable!" Leila says. Lucy nods and grins. I look between my sisters, wondering if they've both lost their minds... Again.

"Are you talking about Jack? He didn't even look at me!"

Leila lifts a finger. "It was the way he *didn't* look at you that was very telling."

Lucy nods, but I get the faint impression she's just as lost as I am at this point. Leila laughs.

"Chessy, he saved my life."

"You should say thank you," Lucy says. Then she gives me a devilish grin. "You should *really* thank him. In a way no one else can."

My cheeks grow hot.

"I can't do that. I made a deal with his ex-wife, remember?"

My sisters groan simultaneously. Leila shifts in the bed and pats my leg.

"Come on, Chessy. You've left your job and moved out from the apartment across the hall. You've given it time. She can't do anything now."

I chew my lip nervously. "But he wouldn't even look at me," I say again, troubled.

Lucy pats my hand. "Wouldn't, or couldn't?"

I suck in a breath. It floods my body with nervous jitters.

Then Leila leans in to mutter a secret to us. "Besides, doesn't he look so cute in his scrubs?"

"Super cute," Lucy agrees. "Some might say hot, even. I know I'm a married woman now, but it doesn't stop me from appreciating how delicious he looked with his biceps bulging out of his shirt like that."

I squeal in shock and stifle a laugh with my hand. Then I look at all the corners of the room in paranoia. If there are cameras and Jack is listening in on this conversation, I'd straight up die. We all would.

Leila turns solemn and takes my hands in hers.

"Chessy," she says. "If the last twenty-four hours have taught me anything, it's that you never know what life is going to throw at you... And Jack is the type of man you want to have in your corner."

"Or your bed," Lucy adds, sounding surprisingly serious for such a cheeky statement.

Leila chuckles. "You and Wyatt look cozy," she remarks mischievously. "Did you two...?"

Lucy's face turns red. She nods shyly. "I was waiting for a moment when I felt like we were crossing a line or something. But that never moment came. In fact, it was so natural, I can't believe we waited this long."

I sigh, knowing exactly what she means.

Of course, flashes of the night Jack and I slept together cross my mind. I can still feel the heat of his eyes taking in my naked body after he tossed me on the bed. My mouth goes dry at the thought.

Leila swivels her head to give me a severe look again, as though my thoughts are broadcasting. "You're going to talk to Jack, right? Promise me you will."

I swallow and wonder how she knew that I was thinking about him again. My first reaction is to argue, but as I study my sister's clammy face, a rush of gratitude floods my veins. She's still alive, and it's because of him.

Whether we get back together or not, he deserves a thank you. It's the very least I can do.

"I will. I promise."

Leila and Lucy smile at me expectantly for a few minutes. I blink back at them.

Leila huffs. "What are you waiting for?"

"He could be in surgery!" I protest, my heart pounding now.

The truth is, I'm not sure I have the strength to face him right now. "Can't it wait a few days?"

When my sisters give me identical deadpan looks, I come up with more excuses.

"I have no idea where he is," I say weakly.

"Let love guide you."

"Love isn't a compass, Leila," I retort.

Lucy snorts. But then her face lights up. *Oh no.* She's just got an idea. "You could go to the reception desk and hijack the intercom. Then make a declaration of love. He'll have to take you back, then."

Leila interrupts with a sound of amazement. "You came up with that just now, didn't you?"

I look from one sister to the other in surprise. I'm the one who usually comes up with the romantic gestures. I'm supposed to be the one with my head in the clouds.

I shake my head, frowning. "He's at work. I'll wait until later. But I will talk to him, I promise."

My sisters are not happy, but they drop the subject and start talking about the babies.

"Have you picked out any names, yet?" Lucy asks.

Leila rolls her eyes. "Blaze wants to call them Luke and Leia. I told him it's illegal."

That piques Lucy's interest. "Is that true?" She's already pulling out her phone as if to find out for herself.

Leila chuckles. "I don't care, it should be. I'm not naming our babies after Star Wars characters."

Their banter fades as I lose myself in my own thoughts.

What will I say to Jack?

Just as I begin to arrange a jigsaw of words in my mind, I get another flashback.

We're in the shower this time, and he's just holding me. We're skin to skin, and the steaming water is beating our connected bodies, drenching us in delicious heat.

My body shivers at the absence of his warmth. It feels so wrong to be apart from him.

I have no idea how I'm going to face him and keep my end of the bargain I made with Beverly.

The truth is there's a very big part of me that hopes we can be together...

Some day.

I'm staring at the coffee machine, wondering why I can't remember how to work it, when two men swagger up to me. I glance in their direction and recognition makes my muscles tense up.

Blaze flashes me a smile and claps a hand on my shoulder. I look up at him. The man is huge. "When do you finish your shift?" he asks.

"I'm done," I say, glancing at the clock. "I started yesterday afternoon."

Blaze and Wyatt exchange looks. "Can we buy you a drink, then?"

I dig my fingers into the tension in the back of my neck with a sigh. "I'd love that, but I'm beat. Rain check?"

Wyatt nods and busies himself with the vending machine, but Blaze edges closer, looking at me like he's about to tell me top secret information. His eyes shoot all around the quiet lobby and I resist the urge to laugh at the sight of this big man being cautious of anything.

"Listen, I owe you a million favors for what you've done," he murmurs into my ear. "And Chessy made us promise not to say anything, but I think you deserve to know."

I keep my eyes fixed on the coffee machine, pretending to be choosing which drink I want, while Blaze continues to talk in a low voice.

"Your ex-wife made some kind of secret deal with her. She isn't allowed to talk to you or see you." He steps back and I look at him. He's sporting a mischievous grin now. "But if she was allowed… We all know there's no question what she would say… or do."

He winks and slaps me on the back.

The words hang in the air and my ears begin to ring at the revelation.

Beverly lied.

A mixture of emotions is swirling in my chest.

I nod to Blaze. "Excuse me… I have to…" I trail off, marching down the hall.

There's a whistle and Blaze shouts, "Go get your woman!"

He's talking about Chessy.

Every molecule in my body is willing me to find her. I want to wrap her up in my arms and smother every inch of her in kisses, but there's another woman I need to see first.

I PULL UP OUTSIDE THE SCHOOL CHARGED WITH adrenaline. My blood is boiling at the fact that Beverly was somehow able to scare off the woman I love. Then she had the audacity to try to convince me she had nothing to do with it.

How could I believe Chessy couldn't handle me and my baggage? Am I really so insecure?

I guess so.

I try to steady my emotions and consider the facts with a level head. There's a deeper layer to be uncovered here, and the only way I'll get to the truth is with gentle persuasion.

I march into the principal's office without knocking. Beverly looks up from her desk, but the only part of her that seems surprised are her brows.

"What are you doing here?" she asks over her glasses.

She's snowed under paperwork and has two dark bags under her eyes.

"I want to see how you are," I say, taking the seat in front of her desk. I keep my voice soft, like I'm speaking to a wild horse. My words make her squint in suspicion, and her shoulders rise.

"I'm fine," she snaps.

I cock my head to the side. "Bev," I say tenderly.

She squirms. I haven't called her Bev since we were married. It must conjure up memories of happier times. Her cheeks grow pink. "I'm... fine," she says, less confident now.

Her eyes drop to the desk and she clears her throat.

For the first time since our divorce, I'm flooded with sympathy.

Only a very unhappy woman could be so determined to cause this much pain and suffering in others. I can't help but take responsibility for her unhappiness.

My insides tangle with guilt.

"Bev, look at me," I say, holding my hands out across the desk. Her hands twitch, but they don't take mine. She lifts watery eyes to meet my stare. I nod to her.

"What's going on?" I ask.

Beverly takes a long, shaky breath, and a single tear leaks out of her left eye.

She avoids my gaze.

"It's Brodie," she says in a strangled voice. "He's not sleeping. He won't stop asking about you, and…" she sniffs, bites her lip. Then wrings her hands. "He's mad at me."

I lift my brows. "Mad at you?"

Beverly snaps her head up to give me cold stare. "It's all *your* fault. He says I'm an evil mom for not letting him eat pizza. He says you let him watch TV in his room. He says you and 'Miss Scott' are going to get married and he wants to live with you two instead."

That's when I see it. The flash behind her furious eyes.

I saw it once before when we were talking about Brodie. I just saw it again.

Fear.

"You're afraid you'll lose Brodie?" I say, the pieces suddenly falling together.

I lean forward in disbelief.

"Bev, you're his *mom*. No matter what happens between us, that isn't going to change."

I reach for her hand, and this time she lets me take it. "You act like it's a competition. It's not. Brodie loves you."

"But he wants to see her," she says desperately. "And that can't happen even if I wanted it to because I've done something, Jack. I've really blown it."

"So, you're going to admit it?" I ask, letting her go and crossing my arms. "You drove her away."

Beverly takes off her glasses and drags her hands over her face with a heavy sigh.

"I thought if I made her disappear, Brodie would move on and we could all just…"

"What?" I ask, annoyance rising. "Play happy families?"

Beverly nips her lip. "I know we're finished. I know that we can't…"

She glances at me, hopeful. I set my jaw and give her a firm look back.

"No, Bev. We can't."

Beverly nods, blinking rapidly now. "Right, well. I don't know what to do. I'm up all night consoling Brodie while he cries over losing his teacher. He hates Mr. Hargreaves—and honestly, I don't blame him—but it's going to take time for me to find a replacement. Even then…"

She ends with a huff and throws her head in her hands with a muffled wail.

I reach into my pocket and rummage around until my fingers close around a small velvet box. My heart hammers as I pull it out and place it on the desk.

Beverly's eyes grow big and round when she sees it. She looks up at me.

"Is that…?"

I nod. She takes a breath.

"And you got it for her?"

I nod again, my stomach knotting itself. "I know it looks like I'm rushing into things, but when you know, you know."

Beverly laces her fingers and presses her palms together so tight, her knuckles go white.

"I'm sorry, Jack. I was willing to do anything not to lose my son. But now he can't stand to be near me. He blames me for everything."

I grit my teeth to stop my retort. Brodie isn't wrong.

She cheated. She rebuffed me. She filed for the divorce. Then she got full custody and refused to let me see Brodie. Worst of all, she used Brodie as a bargaining chip to drive Chessy away.

All of it is her fault. But I'm not going to get her blessing by saying that.

"Drop this ridiculous threat you have hanging over Chessy. Let me go to her. Then Brodie will visit us twice a month and you're free to date whoever you want... So long as he's not a DJ."

Beverly snorts, then she looks at me with scrutiny. "You're really going to marry her?"

I pick up the ring box and rub my thumb across the top in thought. "If she'll have me. You said it yourself; Brodie needs stability. If Chessy and I get married, what's more stable than that?"

Beverly's shoulders rise and fall as she lets out a big, long breath.

"I'm not going to pretend to be happy, because I'm not," she says, rubbing her temples. "But if you're happy, and Brodie starts sleeping through the night again... Then I guess I can be happy too. Someday."

I don't even try to stop the grin from spreading across my face.

Without another word, I dash out of the office and make a run for the car, the sound of my racing heart thumping like a war drum in my ears.

CHESSY

I take the stairs up to my old apartment deep in thought, rehearsing what I'm going to say to Jack. Nothing sounds right for some reason.

Hey, sorry I ghosted you. Thanks for saving my sister.

It sounds bad no matter which way I paint it.

A few steps into the hall, I bump into something hard.

"Ouch!"

"Will you look where you're going?"

I rub my head and blink in surprise. I know that grumpy growl.

My heart is all fluttery as I step back to get a good view. Jack is standing there in his blue scrubs, rubbing his chest. That must have been where my head collided.

We stare at each other for a second.

He's so ridiculously hot. The locks of dark hair falling across his brow are calling to me, willing me to run my fingers through those gorgeous strands and sweep them away from his face.

His eyes sparkle as he takes in my appearance.

"Hey," we say in unison.

A frail voice rings out and startles us both.

"Curse you, young man! What did I say about staying away from this angel?"

I lean to the side to smile at Bob. The old man is standing in his doorway, his stick wobbling in the air as he brandishes it at Jack like a sword.

"It's okay, Bob. I can handle myself," I say, with a laugh.

The old man's expression softens and he nods to me. But he glowers at Jack again as he lowers his stick. "One wrong move... I'll not hesitate to beat you with this, my boy. Even if it's the last thing I do."

"It might be," Jack replies cheekily, giving him a wink.

The man's face turns beetroot red, and he

looks like he's just about to blow a gasket. It takes a lot of coaxing on my end, but he eventually shuffles back into his apartment. The slam of his door is the last we hear of him.

I turn to Jack. He's staring at me like I'm a vision.

"Do you want to come in?" he asks, hesitant.

I open my mouth, but no sound comes out.

"I best not," I finally manage to say. "I shouldn't be here in the first place."

I grind my teeth, trying to ignore the pull to join Jack inside his apartment.

If Beverley finds out I was here... I'm already risking too much, having this conversation in the hall. There's no telling what forbidden lines we'll cross if I actually go inside.

Jack adjusts the waistband of his scrubs and I get a flash of his hip for a second. A rush of excitement soars through me at the sight. Leila is right. He looks *really* good in his scrubs.

Too good.

But we can't do anything about it.

I'm not going back on my deal with Beverly, and I hurt Jack too much. He probably can't trust me again.

"I spoke to Blaze. He told me about the deal you made," Jack says.

What? I gape at him.

"Are you sure you don't want to come in?" he asks. He opens his door and swings it open fully.

I peer inside. The couch is staring at me... Reminding me of the nights we spent making out and watching TV while Brodie slept in the next room.

Oh, how that couch is calling me now!

But nothing has changed. Even if Jack knows about the deal. If he's not hurt beyond repair and still wants to be with me, he'll be dragged through the courts and Brodie will be hurt in the process.

"I can't," I say shaking my head. "I can't come between you and your son. I won't do it."

Jack looks around the empty hall and sighs. Then he shrugs. "Well, here is as good as anywhere, I guess."

He stuffs a hand into his left pocket and pulls something out. Then he goes down on one knee.

"Chessy, will you marry me?"

I blink, rooted to the spot.

Jack opens the little velvet box in his hand to reveal a diamond ring.

The stone catches the light and winks at me.

The thunderous roar of my heartbeat is deafening as I process the scene.

Jack smiles, sensing my panic. "I know I'm supposed to give you some heart-warming speech or make a grand gesture. But I've been on call for twenty hours and my brain is scrambled," he explains. He shakes his hair out of his eyes and looks up at me with a grin.

"I can't let another second go by and not ask…" He pauses. "No, *demand*," he amends firmly, "that you consider being my wife."

"Why the sudden change of heart?" I whisper. "What about your ex-wife?"

Jack shuffles to me, then he wraps an arm around my legs and buries his forehead in my navel. He blows out big puffs of air.

"Please," he says. "I'm so tired." His voice is muted in my shirt. "I'm tired of all the games. The sneaking around. The drama. Marry me. It's the simplest, most logical thing for us to do."

"So, this is purely based on logic?" I ask, humored.

Jack lifts his head to look at me, then he lifts up my shirt and his hot breath steams against my skin. "It's not just logic. There's some biology driving me too."

I close my eyes at the intimacy while he presses his lips to my hip bone. "If you will have me, I will spend the rest of my days worshipping you."

He moans against my stomach and the vibration runs right through me.

I push him back slowly and step away. The look of devastation on his face is almost enough to shatter my heart all over again.

"I don't want you to worship me," I say, kneeling to meet him at his level. I place my hands on his shoulders, squeeze his firm muscles, and put my face in his neck to inhale his rich, masculine scent.

My hands find his hair and smooth it down, then I hold the back of his neck. His muscles tense under me as his hands find my waist. "I know I come with a lot of baggage," he says, searching my eyes. "But you will have my whole heart, and I'll do my very best to make all of the stress worth it."

He slips his hands under my shirt and traces small circles all the way up my sides with his thumbs.

My eyes flutter closed as he handles me like a piece of treasure. So gentle. So tender.

His breaths cloud my neck in heat, and I suck in a breath.

"Am I dreaming?" I wonder aloud.

His hands find my neck and he cups my face.

I open my eyes to see his sparkling at me.

"Is that a yes?" he asks.

Ever since I was a little girl, I've pictured how my future husband would propose. All kinds of scenarios popped into my mind over the years. From moonlight picnics in the park, to candlelit dinners at the fanciest restaurants in the city.

Not one of them looked like this.

Jack and I are exhausted from a long night at the hospital. Our emotions have been through the wringer. But here we are, both of us on our knees, touching and breathing in each other's air in the most sacred, beautiful way.

But this is what real life is like. It's not all glitz and glamor with picture perfect dates and rehearsed speeches delivered in front of thousands of strangers.

It's the simple, quiet moments that no one else is around to see.

It's being enveloped in the arms of the person you love at the end of a long week. It's falling deeper into their soul until you think you cannot fall any further. It's getting caught in a kiss at the very last minute—a kiss that makes everything feel right again.

I press my forehead against Jack's and press my hands on his cheeks.

I love him.

He loves me.

I open my eyes and nuzzle his nose with mine as I plant my lips over his, offering our relationship the kiss of life. He pulls me in for a full body hug.

I am safe. I never want him to let me go again.

"Yes," I whisper against his mouth as we break apart.

Jack grips my hands. "Yes, what?" He searches my eyes as though he's trying to find any sign that I'm not being serious. I lift his shirt and place my hand over his beating heart. His skin is clammy and hard under my fingers. Then I take one of his hands and rest it over my own.

This isn't just another whirlwind romance, or some fanciful dream. In fact, a lot of the past month has been an utter nightmare. But it was all part of the journey to this perfect destination.

He implores me with his eyes. His sweet, blood-shot eyes.

"If you promise to look after my heart…" I whisper. "Then I promise to take care of yours."

Jack kisses me with urgency, rubbing my back and tasting my mouth like a man dying of thirst.

"You have me. All of me," he growls. He squeezes my body and roams with his hands. I hug him with all of my strength. "Then I'm yours. After all," I giggle, "I can't think of anyone better than a surgeon to have my heart. It's in the safest hands."

After slipping the ring onto my finger, Jack roars into my neck, lifts me up, and carries me into his apartment. When the door slams shut, Jack refuses to put me down until we reach the bathroom. He yanks his shirt over his head and drops his pants in haste. Then he leans around the shower curtain to turn on the water.

I eye his beautiful, chiseled body gleaming in sweat.

He gives me another kiss. "Come on, shower time. Then it's straight to bed for a nap. We're going to Atlantic City tonight."

I stifle a laugh. "We're not hanging around, then? No big wedding at the Plaza hotel?" I ask.

Jack stops, his face dropping. "Do you want a big wedding?"

After I take off my clothes, I join him in the tub.

He backs up until we're both under the shower.

The heat of our bodies steams the water.

When we touch skin to skin, everything zings.

I close my eyes with a contented sigh at the overwhelming feeling of being home.

"No. You're right, I don't want to wait. I don't want to wait another second."

"Good," Jack growls, wrapping me up in a bear hug. "Because from now on, you're mine. And there's nothing anyone can do about it so long as you love me, because I'm never letting you go again."

I bury my face in his chest, an explosion of happiness flooding my midriff like a cloud of butterflies. "It's a deal."

EPILOGUE

Chessy

T*hree Months Later*

It's New Year's Eve, and there's an air of excitement at Leila and Blaze's mansion. The staff is moving at top speed, making all the necessary preparations in the kitchen and adding finishing touches in the garden for the party.

Blaze, Jack, and Wyatt are outside grilling steak. Brodie is playing ball with Lucy's new golden retriever.

I walk into the nursery, following the sound of

hushed voices. Lucy and Leila are each holding a baby.

"There they are!" I say, cooing over their sleeping faces.

Leila is glowing. Her hair is silky smooth, her skin is dewy and plump, and she's already lost her baby weight. I guess that's what happens when your husband is a billionaire and he hires a whole team to help you raise two babies.

"Motherhood suits you," I say to her.

She reaches out and places a hand on my little bump. "It suits you too, Chessy boo."

I roll my lips inward and bite against a smile.

"Can you believe it?" Lucy asks, rocking Joshie in her arms. "It doesn't feel like that long ago when we were all single and totally lost in the city."

Leila smiles down at Aubrey, pressing a finger to her baby button nose. "Now look at us. We are so blessed."

She nods to Lucy. "Are you and Wyatt going to have kids?"

Lucy shakes her head. "No. Somebody's gotta play the role of cool Aunt and Uncle," she says, grinning. "But we do have some news…"

Leila and I look at her with wide eyes. "Please don't tell me you're moving to New Zealand," I say, lifting my hands to my open mouth. Lucy chuckles.

"No, but we *are* moving."

Leila gasps in horror.

"Snowdrop Valley. Wyatt's bought a house there and we both just really love the small-town vibe."

I suck in a breath. "Well, I guess it's better than New Zealand."

The three of us walk out into the gardens and join our husbands on the deck.

Husbands.

I glance at the shiny ring on my wedding finger and my heart flutters like it does every time I look at it.

Jack looks up at me and a warm smile breaks out on his face. "Look at that cute bump."

He rubs my swollen stomach and bends to speak to it in a baby voice. "You keep cooking in there, little girl. Daddy loves you *so* much."

Brodie drops the tennis ball he was holding and stomps over to us. "Dad, the baby can't hear you. Silly."

He places his hands on his hips to give Jack a

disapproving stare. It reminds me of Beverly for a second. I chuckle.

"Actually, baby *can* hear him. Baby can hear you too."

Brodie's eyes widen at me. "Really?" He pats my bump gingerly. "Hello, baby. What's for dinner?"

The adults chuckle, but then Brodie soon gets bored by the one-sided conversation and chases after the dog again.

The stars are out, twinkling like millions of tiny jewels. Jack wraps his arm around my waist and nuzzles my neck. "Love you, Mrs. Hart."

I grin and lean my head against his as we look out at the gardens all lit up with fairy lights. "This year, I'm going to be a mom," I say, watching Leila and Blaze each holding a baby and dancing on the deck. They can't keep their eyes off each other.

Jack squeezes my waist. "You already are a mom," he points out.

"Stepmom," I correct him. "I've never been through the newborn baby stage. What if I drop her on her head?"

I'm voicing my deepest fears.

My pregnant brain loves to throw me curve-balls of worst-case scenarios. Jack chuckles.

"You'll be great. You've got so many people who will be with you every step of the way."

Jack positions himself behind me, wrapping me in his arms as I look out at my family. I'm flooded with gratitude.

I look at the babies nestled in the arms of their loving parents, and Brodie running around without a care in the world. Finally, I place my hands over Jack's on my baby bump and smile.

Leila's right. We're blessed.

We kissed a lot of frogs and fought a few dragons, but we finally found our happy ending.

Unlike my sisters and me, the next generation will grow up with attentive, loving parents who will do whatever it takes to make them feel safe and accepted.

I rest my head back on Jack's shoulder with a contented sigh and say a silent thank you to the heavens for everything. I know, without a shadow of a doubt, that we really will live happily ever after.

THE END

. . .

A.N - THANK YOU FOR READING, IF YOU LOVED the story I would really appreciate a nice review. They help me find new readers, which helps me to write more books! And if you want to hear this story come to life and others for free, please follow me on TikTok @lauraburtonauthor

Printed in Great Britain
by Amazon

19426514R00189